He *Was* Jealous.

The thought reverberated through her, but for the first time in two years, what Lucas wanted wasn't a priority. *Her* rules had just changed. From now on it was commitment or nothing.

Her chin firmed. "No. I have an escort. He can take me back to the party."

For a long, tension-filled moment Carla thought Lucas would argue, but then the demanding, possessive gleam was replaced by a familiar control. He nodded curtly, then sent her escort a long, cold look that conveyed a hands-off message that left Carla feeling doubly confused. Lucas didn't want her, but neither did he want anyone else near her.

And if Lucas no longer wanted her, if they really were finished, why had he bothered to search her out?

Dear Reader,

The second story in The Pearl House series centers on Lucas Atraeus and Carla Ambrosi—both gorgeous and high profile, but actually pretty nice beneath all the media hype. They've chosen to keep their passion secret because of the tension and hurt surrounding Constantine Atraeus and Sienna Ambrosi's broken engagement two years previously.

With a wedding for Sienna and Constantine suddenly in the mix, all the obstacles to true love and happiness for Carla and Lucas finally seem to be dissolved. But Lucas has other ideas.

Wary of a past mistake and the fatal attraction to Carla that has seen him breaking every one of the emotional rules he had sworn to live by—and the streak of niceness that makes it hard for him to say no to women and fluffy pets—Lucas needs a foolproof strategy. But no matter what lengths he goes to to finish things with his ex, Lucas can't seem to stay away from an unexpectedly vulnerable Carla. Let's face it, he's dazzled. To the extent that he has to ask himself the question…

What if, this time, the fatal attraction is the real thing?

Fiona Brand

FIONA BRAND

A TANGLED AFFAIR

Harlequin®

Desire

Recycling programs
for this product may
not exist in your area.

ISBN-13: 978-0-373-73179-4

A TANGLED AFFAIR

Copyright © 2012 by Fiona Gillibrand

This edition published by arrangement with Harlequin Books S.A.

For questions and comments about the quality of this book please contact us at Customer_eCare@Harlequin.ca.

® and TM are trademarks of Harlequin Books S.A., used under license. Trademarks indicated with ® are registered in the United States Patent and Trademark Office, the Canadian Trade Marks Office and in other countries.

www.Harlequin.com

Printed in U.S.A.

Books by Fiona Brand

Harlequin Desire

*A Breathless Bride #2154
*A Tangled Affair #2166

Silhouette Intimate Moments

Cullen's Bride #914
Heart of Midnight #977
Blade's Lady #1023
Marrying McCabe #1099
Gabriel West: Still the One #1219
High-Stakes Bride #1403

Silhouette Books

Sheiks of Summer
  "Kismet"

*The Pearl House

Other titles by this author available in ebook format.

FIONA BRAND

lives in the sunny Bay of Islands, New Zealand. Now that both her sons are grown, she continues to love writing books and gardening. After a life-changing time in which she met Christ, she has undertaken study for a bachelor of theology and has become a member of The Order of St. Luke, Christ's healing ministry.

For the Lord. Thank you.

The kingdom of heaven
is like a merchant in search of fine pearls.
—*Matthew* 13:45

One

The vibration of Lucas Atraeus's cell phone disrupted the measured bunch and slide of muscle as he smoothly bench-pressed his own weight.

Gray sweatpants clinging low on narrow hips, broad shoulders bronzed by the early morning light that flooded his private gym, he flowed up from the weight bench and checked the screen of his cell. Few people had his private number; of those only two dared interrupt his early morning workout.

"Si." His voice was curt as he picked up the call.

The conversation with his older brother, Constantine, the CEO of The Atraeus Group, a family-owned multibillion-dollar network of companies, was brief. When he terminated the call, Lucas was grimly aware that within the space of a few seconds a great many things had changed.

Constantine intended to marry in less than a fortnight's

time and, in so doing, he had irretrievably complicated Lucas's life.

The bride, Sienna Ambrosi, was the head of a Sydney-based company, Ambrosi Pearls. She also happened to be the sister of the woman with whom Lucas was currently involved. Although *involved* was an inadequate word to describe the passionate, addictive attraction that had held him in reluctant thrall for the past two years.

The phone vibrated again. Lucas didn't need to see the number to know who the second caller was; his gut reaction was enough. Carla Ambrosi. Long, luscious dark hair, honey-tanned skin, light blue eyes and the kind of taut, curvy body that regularly disrupted traffic and stopped him in his tracks.

Desire kicked, raw and powerful, almost overturning the rigid discipline he had instilled in himself after his girlfriend had plunged to her death in a car accident almost five years ago. Ever since Sophie's death he had pledged not to be ruled by passion or fall into such a destructive relationship ever again.

Lately, a whole two years lately, he had been breaking that rule on a regular basis.

But not anymore.

With an effort of will he resisted the almost overwhelming urge to pick up the call. Seconds later, to his intense relief, the phone fell silent.

Shoving damp, jet-black hair back from his face, he strolled across the pale marble floor to the shower with the loose-limbed power of a natural athlete. In centuries past, his build and physical prowess would have made him a formidable warrior. These days, however, Medinian battle was fought across boardroom tables with extensive share portfolios and gold mined from the arid backbone of the main island.

FIONA BRAND

In the corporate arena, Lucas was undefeated. Relationships, however, had proved somewhat less straightforward.

All benefit from the workout burned away by tension and the fierce, unwanted jolt of desire, he stripped off his clothes, flicked the shower controls and stepped beneath a stream of icy water.

If he did nothing and continued an affair that had become increasingly irresistible and risky, he would find himself engaged to a woman who was the exact opposite of the kind of wife he needed.

A second fatal attraction. A second Sophie.

His only honorable course now was to step away from the emotion and the desire and use the ruthless streak he had hammered into himself when dealing with business acquisitions. He had to form a strategy to end a relationship that had always been destined for disaster, for both of their sakes.

He had tried to finish with Carla once before and failed. This time he would make sure of it.

It was over.

Lucas was finally going to propose.

The glow of a full moon flooded the Mediterranean island of Medinos as Carla Ambrosi brought her rented sports car to a halt outside the forbidding gates of Castello Atraeus.

Giddy delight coupled with nervous tension zinged through her as the paparazzi, on Medinos for her sister's wedding to Constantine Atraeus tomorrow, converged on the tiny sky-blue car. So much for arriving deliberately late and under cover of darkness.

A security guard tapped on her window. She wound the glass down a bare two inches and handed him the cream-colored, embossed invitation to the prewedding dinner.

With a curt nod, he slid the card back through the narrow gap and waved her on.

A flash temporarily blinded her as she inched the tiny rental through the crush, making her wish she had ignored the impulse that had seized her and chosen a sensible, solid four-door sedan instead of opting for a low-slung fun and flimsy sports car. But she had wanted to look breezy and casual, as if she didn't have a care in the world—

A sharp rap on her passenger-side window jerked her head around.

"Ms. Ambrosi, are you aware that Lucas Atraeus arrived in Medinos this morning?"

A heady jolt of anticipation momentarily turned her bones to liquid. She had seen Lucas's arrival on the breakfast news. Minutes later, she had glimpsed what she was sure must be his car as she had strolled along the waterfront to buy coffee and rolls for breakfast.

Flanked by security, the limousine had been hard to miss but, frustratingly, the darkly tinted windows had hidden the occupants from sight. Breakfast forgotten, she had both called and texted Lucas. They had arranged to meet but, frustratingly, a late interview request from a popular American TV talk-show host had taken that time slot. With Ambrosi's new collection due for release in under a week, the opportunity to use the publicity surrounding Sienna's wedding to showcase their range and mainstream Ambrosi's brand had been pure gold. Carla had hated canceling but she had known that Lucas, with his clinical approach to business, would understand. Besides, she was seeing him tonight.

Another camera flash made the tension headache she had been fighting since midafternoon spike out of control. The headache was a sharp reminder that she needed to slow down, chill out, de-stress. Difficult to do with the type A personality her doctor had diagnosed just over two years ago, along with a stomach ulcer.

The doctor, who also happened to be a girlfriend, had

advised her to lose her controlling, perfectionist streak, to stop micromanaging every detail of her life including her slavish need to color coordinate her wardrobe and plan her outfits a week in advance. Her approach to relationships was a case in point. Her current system of spreadsheet appraisal was hopelessly punitive. How could she find Mr. Right if no one ever qualified for a second date? Stress was a killer. She needed to loosen up, have some fun, maybe even consider actually sleeping with someone, before she ended up with even worse medical complications.

Carla had taken Jennifer at her word. A week later she had met Lucas Atraeus.

"Ms. Ambrosi, now that your sister is marrying Constantine, is there any chance of resurrecting your relationship with Lucas?"

Jaw tight, Carla continued to inch forward, her heart pounding at the reporter's intrusive question, which had been fired at her like a hot bullet.

And which had been eating at her ever since Sienna had broken the news two weeks ago that she had agreed to marry Constantine.

Tonight, though, she was determined not to resent the questions or the attention. After two years of avoiding being publicly linked with Lucas after the one night the press claimed they had spent together, she was now finally free to come clean about the relationship.

The financial feud that had torn the Atraeus and Ambrosi families apart, and the grief of her sister's first broken engagement to Constantine, were now in the past. Sienna and Constantine had their happy ending. Now, tonight, she and Lucas could finally have theirs.

A throaty rumble presaged the glare of headlights as a gleaming, muscular black car glided in behind her.

Lucas.

Her heart slammed against the wall of her chest. He was staying at the *castello,* which meant he had probably been at a meeting in town and was just returning. Or he could have driven to the small town house she and Sienna and their mother were renting in order to collect her. The possibility of the second option filled her with relieved pleasure.

A split second later the way ahead was clear as the media deserted her in favor of clustering around Lucas's Maserati. Automatically, Carla's foot depressed the accelerator, sending her small sports car rocketing up the steep, winding slope. Scant minutes later, she rounded a sweeping bend and the spare lines of the *castello* she had only ever seen in magazine articles jumped into full view.

The headlights of the Maserati pinned her as she parked on the smooth sweep of gravel fronting the colonnaded entrance. Feeling suddenly, absurdly vulnerable, she retrieved the flame-red silk clutch that matched her dress and got out of the car.

The Maserati's lights winked out, plunging her into comparative darkness as she closed her door and locked the car.

She started toward the Maserati, still battling the aftereffects of the bright halogen lights. The sensitivity of her eyes was uncomfortably close to a symptom she had experienced two months ago when she had contracted a virus while holidaying with Lucas in Thailand.

Instead of the romantic interlude she had so carefully planned and which would have generated the proposal she wanted, Lucas had been forced into the role of nursemaid. On her return home, when she had continued to feel off-color, further tests had revealed that the stomach ulcer she thought she had beaten had flared up again.

The driver's side door of the car swung open. Her pulse rate rocketed off the charts. Finally, after a day of anxious waiting, they would meet.

Meet.

Her mouth went dry at a euphemism that couldn't begin to describe the explosive encounters that, over the past year, had become increasingly intense.

The reporter at the gate had put his finger on an increasingly tender and painful pulse. Resurrect her relationship with Lucas?

Technically, she was not certain they had ever had anything as balanced as a relationship. Her attempt to create a relaxed, fun atmosphere with no stressful strings had not succeeded. Lucas had seemed content with brief, crazily passionate interludes, but she was not. As hard as she had tried to suppress her type A tendencies and play the glamorous, carefree lover, she had failed. Passion was wonderful, but she *liked* to be in control, to personally dot every *i* and cross every *t*. For Carla, leaving things "open" had created even more stress.

Heart pounding, she started toward the car. The gown she had bought with Lucas in mind was unashamedly spectacular and clung where it touched. Split down one side, it revealed the long, tanned length of her legs. The draped neckline added a sensual Grecian touch to the swell of her breasts and also hid the fact that she had lost weight over the past few weeks.

Her chest squeezed tight as Lucas climbed out of the car with a fluid muscularity she would always recognize.

She drank in midnight eyes veiled by inky lashes, taut cheekbones, the faintly battered nose, courtesy of two seasons playing professional rugby; his strong jaw and firm, well-cut mouth. Despite the sleek designer suit and the ebony seal ring that gleamed on one finger, Lucas looked somewhat less than civilized. A graphic image of him naked and in her bed, his shoulders muscled and broad, his skin dark against crisp white sheets, made her stomach clench.

His gaze captured hers and the idea that they could keep the chemistry that exploded between them a secret until after the wedding died a fiery death. She wanted him. She had waited two years, hamstrung by Sienna's grief at losing Constantine. She loved her sister and was fiercely loyal. Dating the younger and spectacularly better looking Atraeus brother when Sienna had been publicly dumped by Constantine would have been an unconscionable betrayal.

Tonight, she and Lucas could publicly acknowledge their desire to be together. Not in a heavy-handed, possessive way that would hint at the secretive liaison that had disrupted both of their lives for the past two years, but with a low-key assurance that would hint at the future.

As Ambrosi's public relations "face," she understood exactly how this would be handled. There would be no return to the turgid headlines that had followed their first passionate night together. There would be no announcements, no fanfare…at least, not until after tomorrow's wedding.

Despite the fact that her strappy high heels, a perfect color match for the dress, made her more than a little unstable on the gravel, she jogged the last few yards and flung herself into Lucas's arms.

The clean scent that was definitively Lucas, mingled with the masculine, faintly exotic undernote of sandalwood, filled her nostrils, making her head spin. Or maybe it was the delight of simply touching him again after a separation that had run into two long months.

The cool sea breeze whipped long silky coils of hair across her face as she lifted up on her toes. Her arms looped around his neck, her body slid against his, instantly responding to his heat, the utter familiarity of broad shoulders and sleek, hard-packed muscle. His sudden intake of breath, the unmistakable feel of him hardening against the soft contours of her belly filled her with mindless relief.

Ridiculous tears blurred her vision. This was so *not* playing it cool, but it had been two months since she had touched, kissed, made love to her man. Endless days while she had waited for the annoying, debilitating ulcer—clear evidence that she had not coped with her unresolved emotional situation—to heal. Long weeks while she had battled the niggling anxiety that had its roots in the disastrous bout of illness in Thailand, as if she was waiting for the next shoe to drop.

She realized that one of the reasons she had not told Lucas about the complications following the virus was that she had been afraid of the outcome. Over the years he had dated a string of gorgeous, glamorous women so she usually took great care that he only ever saw her at her very best. There had been nothing pretty or romantic about the fever that had gripped her in Thailand. There had been even less glamour surrounding her hospital stay in Sydney.

Lucas's arms closed around her, his jaw brushed her cheek sending a sensual shiver the length of her spine. Automatically, she leaned into him and lifted her mouth to his, but instead of kissing her, he straightened and unlooped her arms from his neck. Cold air filled the space between them.

When she moved to close the frustrating distance he gripped her upper arms.

"Carla." His voice was clipped, the Medinian accent smoothed out by the more cosmopolitan overtones of the States, but still dark and sexy enough to send another shiver down her spine. "I tried to ring you. Why didn't you pick up the call?"

The mundane question, the edged tone pulled her back to earth with a thump. "I switched my phone off while I was being interviewed then I put it on charge."

But it had only been that way for about an hour. When she had left the private villa she was sharing with her mother and Sienna, she had grabbed the phone and dropped it in her purse. His hands fell away from her arms, leaving a palpable chill in place of the warm imprint of his palms. Extracting the phone from her clutch, she checked the screen and saw that, in her hurry, she had forgotten to turn it on.

She activated the phone, and instantly the missed calls registered on the screen. "Sorry," she said coolly. "Looks like I forgot to turn it back on."

She frowned at his lack of response. With an effort of will, she controlled the unruly emotions that had had the temerity to explode out of their carefully contained box and dropped the phone back in her clutch. So, okay, this was subtext for "let's play it cool."

Fine. Cool she could do, but not doormat. "I'm sorry I missed meeting you earlier but you've been here most of the day. If you'd wanted we could have met for lunch."

A discreet thunk snapped Carla's head around. Automatically, she tracked the unexpected sound and movement as the passenger door of the Maserati swing open.

Not male. Which ruled out her first thought, that the second occupant of the Maserati, hidden from her view by darkly tinted windows, was one of the security personnel who sometimes accompanied Lucas.

Not male. Female.

Out of nowhere her heart started to hammer. A series of freeze frames flickered: silky dark hair caught in a perfect chignon; a smooth, elegant body encased in shimmering, pale pearlized silk.

She went hot then cold, then hot again. She had the abrupt sensation that she was caught in a dream. A *bad* dream.

She and Lucas had an agreement whereby they could date others in order to distract the press and preserve the privacy she had insisted upon. But not here, not now.

Jerkily, Carla completed the movement she realized Lucas wanted from her: she stepped back.

She focused on his face, for the first time fully absorbing the remoteness of his dark gaze. It was the same cool neutrality she had seen on the odd occasion when they had been together and he'd had to take a work call.

The throbbing in her head increased, intensified by a shivery sensitivity that swept her spine. Her fingers tightened on her clutch as she resisted the sudden, childish urge to hug away the chill.

She drew an impeded breath. Another woman? She had not seen that coming.

Her mind worked frantically. No. It couldn't be.

But, if she hadn't felt that moment of heated response she *could* almost think that Lucas—

Emotion flickered in his gaze, gone almost before she registered it. "I believe you've met Lilah."

Recognition followed as Lilah turned and the light from the portico illuminated delicate cheekbones and exotic eyes. "Of course." She acknowledged Ambrosi's spectacularly talented head designer with a stiff nod.

Of course she knew Lilah, and Lilah knew her.

And all about her situation with Lucas, if she correctly interpreted the sympathy in Lilah's eyes.

Confusion rocked her again. How dare Lucas confide their secret to anyone without her permission? And Lilah Cole wasn't just anyone. The Coles had worked for Ambrosi's for as long as Carla could remember. Carla's grandfather, Sebastien, had employed Lilah's mother in Broome. Lilah, herself, had worked for Ambrosi for the past five years, the last two as their head designer, creating some of their most exquisite jewelry.

Lilah's smile and polite greeting were more than a little wary as she closed the door of the Maserati and strolled around the front of the car to join them.

The sudden uncomfortable silence was broken as the front

door of the *castello* was pushed wide. Light flared across the smooth expanse of gravel, the soft strains of classical music filtered through the haze of shock that still held Carla immobile.

A narrow, well-dressed man Carla recognized as Tomas, Constantine's personal assistant, spoke briefly in Medinian and motioned them all inside.

With a curt nod, Lucas indicated that both Carla and Lilah precede him. Feeling like an automaton, Carla walked toward the broad steps, no longer caring that the gravel was ruining her shoes. Exquisite confections she had chosen with Lucas in mind—along with every other item of jewelry and clothing she was wearing tonight, including her lingerie.

With each step she could feel the distance between them, a mystifying cold impersonality, growing by the second. When his hand landed in the small of Lilah's back, steadying her as she hitched up her gown with a poised, unutterably graceful movement, Carla's heart squeezed on a pang of misery. In those few seconds she finally acknowledged the insidious fear that had coexisted with her need to be with Lucas for almost two years.

She knew how dangerous Lucas was in business. As Constantine's right hand, by necessity he had to be coldly ruthless.

The other shoe had finally dropped. She had just been smoothly, ruthlessly dumped.

Two

Tucking a glossy strand of dark hair behind her ear—hair that suddenly seemed too lush and unruly for a formal family occasion—Carla stepped into the disorienting center of what felt like a crowd.

In reality there were only a handful of people present in the elegant reception room: Tomas and members of the Atraeus family including Constantine, his younger brother, Zane, and Lucas's mother, Maria Therese. To one side, Sienna was chatting with their mother, Margaret Ambrosi.

Sienna, wearing a sleek ivory dress and already looking distinctly bridal, was the first to greet her. The quick hug, the moment of warmth, despite the fact that they had spent most of the morning going over the details of the wedding together, made Carla's throat lock.

Sienna gripped her hands, frowning. "Are you okay? You look a little pale."

"I'm fine, just a little rushed and I didn't expect the media ambush at the gates." Carla forced a bright smile. "You know me. I do thrive on publicity, but the reporters were like a pack of wolves."

Constantine, tall and imposing, greeted her with a brief hug, the gesture conveying her new status as a soon-to-be member of Medinos's most wealthy, powerful family. He frowned as he released her. "Security should have kept them at bay."

His expression was remote, his light gray gaze controlled, belying the primitive fact that he had used financial coercion and had even gone so far as kidnapping Sienna to get his former fiancée back.

"The security was good." Carla hugged her mother, fighting the ridiculous urge to cling like a child. If she did that she would cry, and she refused to cry in front of Lucas.

A waiter offered champagne. As she lifted the flute from the tray her gaze clashed with Lucas's. Her fingers tightened reflexively on the delicate stem. The message in his dark eyes was clear.

Don't talk. Don't make trouble.

She took a long swallow of the champagne. "Unfortunately, the line of questioning the press took was disconcerting. Although I'm sure that when Lucas arrived with Lilah any misconceptions were cleared up."

Sienna's expression clouded. "Don't tell me they're trying to resurrect that old story about you and Lucas?"

Carla controlled her wince reflex at the use of the word *resurrect*. "I guess it's predictable that now that you and Constantine have your happy ending, the media are looking to generate something out of nothing."

Sienna lifted a brow. "So, do they need a medic down at the gates?"

"Not this time." Lucas frowned as Carla took another

long swallow of champagne. "Don't forget I was the original target two years ago, not the media."

And suddenly the past was alive between them, vibrating with hurtful accusations and misunderstandings she thought they had dealt with long ago. The first night of unplanned and irresistible passion they'd shared, followed by the revelation of the financial deal her father had leveraged on the basis of Sienna's engagement to Constantine. Lucas's accusation that Carla was more interested in publicity and her career than she had been in him.

Carla forced herself to loosen her grip on the stem of her glass. "But then the media are so very fascinated by your private life, aren't they?"

A muscle pulsed along the side of his jaw. "Only when someone decides to feed them information."

The flat statement, correct as it was, stung. Two years ago, hurt by his comments, she had reacted by publicly stating that she had absolutely no interest in being pursued by Lucas. The story had sparked weeks of uncomfortable conjecture for them both.

Sienna left them to greet more arrivals. Her anger under control, Carla examined the elegant proportions of the reception room, the exquisite marble floors and rich, Italianate decor. "And does that thought keep you awake at night?"

Lucas's gaze flared at her deliberate reference to the restless passion for her that he had once claimed kept him awake at nights. "I'm well used to dealing with the media."

"A shame there isn't a story. It could have benefited Ambrosi's upcoming product launch." She forced a brilliant smile. "You know what they say, any publicity is good publicity. Although in this case, I'm sure the story wouldn't be worth the effort, especially when it would involve dragging *my* private life through the mud."

Lucas's expression shuttered, the fire abruptly gone. "Then I suggest you sleep easy. *I* don't kiss and tell."

The sense of disorientation she had felt the past few minutes evaporated in a rush of anger. "Or commit to relationships."

"You were the one who set the ground rules."

Suddenly Lucas seemed a lot closer. "You know I had no other option."

His expression was grim. "The truth is always an option."

Her chin jerked up. "I was protecting Sienna and my family. What was I supposed to do? Turn up with you at Mom and Dad's house for Sunday dinner and admit that I was—"

"Sleeping with me?"

The soft register of his voice made her heart pound. Every nerve in her body jangled at his closeness, the knowledge that he was just as aware of her as she was of him. "I was about to say dating an Atraeus."

Sienna returned from her hostess duties to step neatly between them. "Time out, children."

Lucas lifted a brow, his mouth quirking in the wry half smile that regularly made women go weak at the knees. "My apologies."

As Constantine joined them, Lucas drew Lilah into the circle. "I know I don't need to introduce Lilah."

There was a moment of polite acknowledgment and brief handshakes as Lilah was accepted unconditionally into the Atraeus fold. The process of meeting Maria Therese was more formal and underlined a salient and well-publicized fact. Atraeus men didn't take their women home to meet their families on a casual basis. To her best knowledge, until now, Lucas had never taken a girlfriend home to meet his mother.

Lucas's *girlfriend.*

Lilah was smiling, her expression contained but lit with an unmistakable glow.

A second salient fact made Carla stiffen. A few months ago, while stuck overnight together at a sales expo in Europe, she and Lilah had discussed the subject of relationships. At age twenty-nine, despite possessing the kind of sensual dark-haired, white-skinned beauty that riveted male attention, Lilah was determinedly single.

She had told Carla a little of her background, which included a single mother, a solo grandmother and ongoing financial hardship. Born illegitimate, Lilah had early on given herself a rule. No sex before marriage. There was no way she was going to be left holding a baby.

While Carla had stressed about finding Mr. Right, Lilah was calmly focused on marrying him, her approach methodical and systematic. She had moved on a step from Carla's idea of a spreadsheet and had developed a list of qualifying attributes as precise and unwavering as an employment contract. Also, unlike Carla, Lilah had *saved* herself for marriage. She was that twenty-first century paragon: a virgin.

The simple fact that she was on Medinos with Lucas, thousands of miles from her Sydney apartment and rigorous work schedule, spoke volumes.

Lilah did not date. Carla knew that she occasionally accompanied a gay neighbor to his professional dinners and had him escort her to charity functions she supported. But their relationship was purely friendship, which suited them both. That was all.

Carla took another gulp of champagne. Her stomach clenched because the situation was suddenly blindingly obvious.

Lilah was dating Lucas because she had chosen him. He was her intended husband.

Anger churned in Carla's stomach and stiffened her spine. She and Lucas had conducted their relationship based on a set of rules that was the complete opposite of everything that

Lilah was holding out for: no strings, strictly casual and, because of the family feud, in secrecy.

An enticing, convenient arrangement for a man who clearly had never had any intention of offering *her* marriage.

Waiters served more chilled champagne and trays of tiny, exquisite canapés. Carla forced herself to eat a tiny pastry case filled with a delicate seafood mousse. She continued to sip her way through the champagne, which loosened the tightness of her throat but couldn't wash away the deepening sense of hurt.

Lilah Cole was beautiful, elegant and likable, but nothing could change the fact that Lilah's easy acceptance into the Atraeus fold should have been *her* moment.

The party swelled as more family and friends arrived. Abandoning her champagne flute on a nearby sideboard, Carla joined the movement out onto a large stone balcony overlooking the sea.

Feeling awkward and isolated amidst the crowd, she threaded her way through the revelers to the parapet and stared out at the expansive view. The breeze gusted, laced with the scent of the sea, sending coils of hair across her cheeks and teasing at the flimsy silk of her dress, briefly exposing more leg than she had planned.

Lucas's gaze burned over her, filled with censure, not the desire that had sizzled between them for the past two years.

Cheeks burning, she snapped her dress back into place, her mood plummeting further as Lilah joined Lucas. Despite the breeze, Lilah's hair was neat and perfect, her dress subtly sensual with a classic pureness of line that suddenly made Carla feel cheap and brassy, all sex and dazzle against Lilah's demure elegance. Her cheeks grew hotter as she considered what she was wearing under the red silk. Again, nothing with any degree of subtlety. Every flimsy stitch was designed to entice.

She had taken a crazy risk in dressing so flamboyantly, practically begging for the continuation of their relationship. After the distance of the past two months she should have had more sense than to wear her heart on her sleeve. Jerking her gaze away, she tried to concentrate on the moon sliding up over the horizon, the churning floodlit water below the *castello*.

A cool gust of wind sent more hair whipping around her cheeks. Temporarily blinded, she snatched at her billowing hemline. Strong fingers gripped her elbow, steadying her. Heart-stoppingly familiar dark eyes clashed with hers. Not Lucas, Zane Atraeus.

"Steady. I've got you. Come over here, out of the wind before we lose you over the side."

Zane's voice was deep, mild and low-key, more American than Medinian, thanks to his Californian mother and upbringing. With his checkered, illegitimate past and lady-killer reputation, Zane was, of the three brothers, definitely the most approachable and she wondered a little desperately why she hadn't been able to fall for him instead of Lucas. "Thanks for the rescue."

He sent her an enigmatic look. "Damsels in distress are always my business."

The warmth in her cheeks flared a little brighter. The suspicion that Zane wasn't just talking about the wind, that he knew about her affair with Lucas, coalesced into certainty.

He positioned her in the lee of a stone wall festooned with ivy. "Can I get you a drink?"

A reckless impulse seized Carla as she glanced across at Lucas. "Why not?"

With his arm draped casually across the stone parapet behind Lilah, his stance was male and protective, openly claiming Lilah as his, although he wasn't touching her in any way.

Unbidden, a small kernel of hope flared to life at that

small, polite distance. Ten minutes ago, Carla had been certain they were an established couple; that to be here, at a family wedding, Lucas would have had to have slept with Lilah. Now she was abruptly certain they had not yet progressed to the bedroom. There was a definite air of restraint underpinning the glow on Lilah's face, and despite his possessive stance, Lucas was preserving a definite distance.

A waiter swung by. Zane handed her a flute of champagne. "Do you think they've slept together?"

Carla's hand jerked at the question. Champagne splashed over her fingers. She dragged her gaze from the clean line of Lucas's profile and glanced at Zane. His expression was oddly grim, his jaw set. "I don't know why you're asking me that question."

Zane, who hadn't bothered with champagne, gave her a steady look, and humiliation curled through her. He knew.

Carla wondered a little wildly how he had found out and if everyone on the balcony knew that she was Lucas's ditched ex.

Zane's expression was dismissive. "Don't worry, it was a lucky guess."

Relief flooded her as she swallowed a mouthful of champagne. A few seconds later her head began to spin and she resolved not to drink any more.

Zane's attention was no longer on her; it was riveted on Lilah and realization hit. She wasn't the only one struggling here. "You want Lilah."

The grim anger she had glimpsed winked out of existence. "If I was in the market for marriage, maybe."

"Which, I take it, you're not."

Zane's dark gaze zeroed in on hers, but Carla realized he still barely logged her presence. "No. Are you interested in art?"

Carla blinked at the sudden change of subject. "Yes."

"If you want out of this wind, I'll be happy to show you the rogue's gallery."

She had glimpsed the broad gallery that housed the Atraeus family portraits, some painted by acknowledged masters, but hadn't had time to view them. "I would love to take a closer look at the family portraits."

Anything to get her off the balcony. "Just do me one favor. Put your arm around my waist."

"And make it look good?"

Carla's chin jerked up a fraction. "If you don't mind."

The unflattering lack of reaction to her suggestion should have rubbed salt into the wound, but Carla was beyond caring. She was dying by inches but she was determined not to be any more tragic than she had to be.

Lucas's gaze burned over her as she handed her drink to a waiter then allowed Zane's arm to settle around her waist. As they strolled past Lucas, she was forcibly struck by the notion that he was jealous.

Confusion rocked her. She hadn't consciously set out to make Lucas jealous; her main concern from the moment she had realized that Lucas and Lilah were together had been self-preservation. Lucas being jealous made no sense unless he still wanted her, and how could that be when he had already chosen another woman?

Carla was relieved when Zane dropped his arm the second they were out of sight of the balcony. After a short walk through flagged corridors, they entered the gallery. Along one wall, arched windows provided spectacular views of the moonlit sea. The opposite wall was softly lit and lined with exquisite paintings.

The tingling sense of alarm, as if at some level she was aware of Lucas's displeasure, continued as they strolled past rank after rank of gorgeous rich oils. Most had been painted pre-1900s, before the once wealthy and noble Atraeus family had fallen on hard times. Lucas's grandfather, after discovering an obscenely rich gold mine, had since purchased most of the paintings back from private collections and museums.

The men were clearly of the Atraeus bloodline, with strong jaws and aquiline profiles. The women, almost without exception, looked like Botticelli angels: beautiful, demure, virginal.

Zane paused beside a vibrant painting of an Atraeus ancestor who looked more like a pirate than a noble lord. His lady was a serene, quiet dove with a steely glint in her eye. With her long, slanting eyes and delicate bones, the woman bore an uncanny resemblance to Lilah. "As you can see it's a mixture of sinners and saints. It seemed that the more dissolute and marauding the Atraeus male, the more powerful his desire for a saint."

Carla heard the measured tread of footsteps. Her heart sped up because she was almost sure it was Lucas. "And is that what Atraeus men are searching for today?"

Zane shrugged. "I can't speak for my brothers. I'm not your typical Atraeus male."

Her jaw tightened. "But the idea of a pure, untouched bride still has a certain appeal."

"Maybe." He sent her a flashing grin that made him look startlingly like the Atraeus pirate in the painting. "Although, I'm always willing to be convinced that a sinner is the way to go."

"Because that generally means no commitment, right?"

Zane's dark brows jerked together. "How did we get on to commitment?"

Carla registered the abrupt silence as if whoever had just entered the gallery had seen them and stopped.

Her heart slammed in her chest as she caught Lucas's reflection in one of the windows. On impulse, she stepped close to Zane and tilted her head back, the move flirtatious and openly provocative. She was playing with fire, because Zane had a reputation that scorched.

Lucas would be furious with her. If he *was* jealous, her behavior would probably kill any feelings he had left for her, but she was beyond caring. He had hurt her too badly for her to pull back now. "If that's an invitation, the answer is yes."

Zane's gaze registered unflattering surprise.

Minor detail, because Lucas was now walking toward them. Gritting her teeth, she wound her finger in Zane's tie, applying just enough pressure that his head lowered until his mouth was mere inches from hers.

His gaze was disarmingly neutral. "I know what you're up to."

"You could at least be tempted."

"I'm trying."

"Try harder."

"Damn, you're type A. No wonder he went for Lilah."

Carla's fingers tightened on his tie. "Is it that obvious?"

"Only to me. And that's because I'm a control freak myself."

"I am *not* a control freak."

He unwound her fingers from his tie. "Whatever you say."

Cut adrift by Zane's calm patience, Carla had no choice but to step back and in so doing almost caromed into Lucas.

She flinched at the fiery trail of his gaze over the shadow of her cleavage, her mouth, the impression of heat and desire. If Zane hadn't been there she was almost certain he would have pulled her close and kissed her.

Lucas's expression was shuttered. "What are you up to?"

Carla didn't try to keep the bitterness out of her voice. "*I'm* not up to anything. Zane was showing me the paintings."

"Careful," Zane intervened, his gaze on Lucas. "Or I

might think you have a personal interest in Carla, and that couldn't possibly be, since you're dating the lovely Lilah."

A sharp pang went through Carla at the tension vibrating between the brothers, shifting undercurrents she didn't understand.

Spine rigid, she kept her gaze firmly on Zane's jaw. She hadn't liked behaving like that, but at least she had proved that Lucas did still want her. Although the knowledge was a bitter pill, because his reaction repeated a pattern that was depressingly familiar. In establishing a stress-free liaison with him based on her rules, she had somehow negotiated herself out of the very things she needed most: love, companionship and commitment.

Lucas had wanted her for two years, but that was all. The relationship had struggled to progress out of the bedroom. Even when she had finally gotten him to Thailand for a whole four-day minibreak, the longest period of time they had ever spent together, the plan had crashed and burned because she had gotten sick.

She wondered in what way she was lacking that Lucas didn't want a full relationship with her? That instead of allowing them to grow closer, he had kept her at an emotional arm's length and gone to Lilah for the very things that Carla needed from him.

She glanced apologetically at Zane in an effort to defuse the tension. "It's okay, Lucas and I are old news. If there was anything more we would be together now."

"Whereas marriage *is* Lilah's focus," Zane said softly.

Lucas frowned. "Back off, Zane."

Confusion gripped Carla along with another renegade glimmer of hope at Lucas's reaction. She was tired of thinking about everything that had gone wrong, but despite that, her mind grabbed on to the notion that maybe all he was doing *was* dating Lilah on a casual basis. Just because Lilah wanted marriage didn't necessarily mean she would get what she wanted.

Grimly, she forced herself to study the Atraeus bride in the painting again. It was the perfect reality check.

Her pale, demure gown was the epitome of all things virginal and pure. Nothing like Carla's flaming red silk dress, with its enticing glimpse of cleavage and leg. The serene eighteenth-century bride was no doubt every man's secret dream. A perfect wife, without a flirty bone in her body. Or a stress condition.

Lucas's gaze sliced back to Carla. "I'll take you back to the party. Dinner will be served in about fifteen minutes."

He *was* jealous.

The thought reverberated through her, but for the first time in two years what Lucas wanted wasn't a priority. *Her* rules had just changed. From now on it was commitment or nothing.

Her chin firmed. "No. I have an escort. Zane will take me back to the party."

For a long, tension-filled moment Carla thought Lucas would argue, but then the demanding, possessive gleam was replaced by a familiar control. He nodded curtly then sent Zane a long, cold look that conveyed a hands-off message that left Carla feeling doubly confused. Lucas didn't want her, but neither did he want Zane anywhere near her.

And if Lucas no longer wanted her, if they really were finished, why had he bothered to search her out?

Three

Lucas Atraeus strode into his private quarters and snapped the door closed behind him. Opening a set of French doors, he stepped out onto his balcony. The wind buffeted the weathered stone parapet and whipped night-dark hair around the obdurate line of his jaw. He tried to focus on the steady roar of the waves pounding the cliff face beneath and the stream of damp, salty air, while he waited for the self-destructive desire to reclaim Carla to dissolve.

The vibration of his cell phone drew him back inside. Sliding the phone out of his pocket, he checked the screen. Lilah. No doubt wondering where he was.

Jaw clenched, he allowed the call to go through to his voice mail. He couldn't stomach talking to Lilah right at that moment with his emotions still raw and his thoughts on another woman. Besides, with a relationship based on a few phone calls and a couple of conversations, most of them purely work based, they literally had nothing to say to each other.

The call terminated. Lucas found himself staring at a newspaper he had tossed down on the coffee table, the one he had read on the night flight from New York to Medinos. The paper was open at the society pages and a grainy shot of Carla in her capacity as the "face" of Ambrosi Pearls, twined intimately close with a rival millionaire businessman.

Picking up the newspaper, he reread the caption that hinted at a hot affair.

He had been away for two months but by all accounts she had not missed him.

Tossing the newspaper down on the coffee table, he strode back out onto the balcony. Before he could stop himself, he had punched in her number on his phone.

Calling her now made no kind of sense.

He held the sleek phone pressed to his ear and forced himself to remember the one overriding reason he should never have touched Carla Ambrosi.

Grimly, he noted that the hit of old grief and sharp-enough-to-taste guilt still wasn't powerful enough to bury the impulse to involve himself even more deeply in yet another fatal attraction.

When he had met Carla, somehow he had stepped away from the rigid discipline he had instilled in himself after Sophie's death.

The car accident hadn't been his fault, but he was still haunted by the argument that had instigated Sophie's headlong dash in her sports car after he had found out that she had aborted his child.

Sophie had been beautiful, headstrong and adept at winding him around her little finger. He should have stopped her, taken the car keys. He should have controlled the situation. It had been his responsibility to protect her, and he had failed.

They should never have been together in the first place.

They had been all wrong for each other. He had been disciplined, work focused and family orientated. Sophie had skimmed along the surface of life, thriving on bright lights, parties and media attention. Even the manner in which Sophie had died had garnered publicity and had been perceived in certain quarters as glamorous.

The ring tone continued. His fingers tightened on the cell. Carla had her phone with her; she should have picked up by now.

Unless she was otherwise occupied. *With Zane.*

His stomach clenched at the image of Carla, mouthwateringly gorgeous in red, her fingers twined in Zane's tie, poised for a kiss he had interrupted.

He didn't trust Zane. His younger brother had a reputation with women that literally burned.

The call went through to voice mail. Carla's voice filled his ear.

Despite the annoyance that gripped him that Carla had decided to ignore his call, Lucas was riveted by the velvet-cool sound of the recorded message. The brisk, businesslike tone so at odds with Carla's ultrasexy, ultrafeminine appearance and which never failed to fascinate.

During the two months he had been in the States he had refrained from contacting Carla. He had needed to distance himself from a relationship that during an intense few days in Thailand had suddenly stepped over an invisible boundary and become too gut-wrenchingly intimate. Too like his relationship with Sophie.

Carla, who was surprisingly businesslike and controlled when it came to communication, had left only one text and a single phone message to which he had replied. A few weeks ago he had seen her briefly, from a distance, at her father's funeral, but they hadn't spoken.

That was reason number two not to become involved with Carla.

The ground rules for their relationship had been based on what she had wanted: a no-strings fun fling, carried out in secret because of the financial scandal that had erupted between their two families.

Secrecy was not Lucas's thing, but since he had never planned on permanency he hadn't seen any harm in going along with Carla's plan. He had been based in the States, Carla was in Sydney. A relationship wasn't possible even if he had wanted one.

The line hummed expectantly.

Irritated with himself for not having done it sooner, Lucas terminated the call.

Grimly, he stared at the endless expanse of sea, the faint curve of the horizon. Carla not picking up the call was the best-case scenario. If she had, he was by no means certain he could have maintained his ruthless facade.

The problem was that, as tough and successful as he was in business, when it came to women his track record was patchy.

As an Atraeus he was expected to be coolly dominant. Despite the years he had spent trying to mold himself into the strong silent type who routinely got his way, he had not achieved Constantine's effortless self-possession. Little kids and fluffy dogs still targeted him; women of all ages gravitated to him as if they had no clue about his reputation as The Atraeus Group's key hatchet man.

Despite the long list of companies he had streamlined or clinically dismantled, he couldn't forget that he had not been able to establish any degree of control over his relationship with Sophie.

Jaw taut, Lucas padded inside. He barely noticed the

warm glow of lamplight, the richness of exquisite antiques and jewel-bright carpets.

His gaze zeroed in on the newspaper article again. A hot pulse of jealously burned through him as he studied the Greek millionaire who had his arm around Carla's waist.

Alex Panopoulos, an archrival across the boardroom table and a well-known playboy.

Given the limited basis of Lucas's relationship with Carla, they had agreed it had to be open; they were both free to date others. Like Lucas, Carla regularly dated as part of her career, although so far Lucas had not been able to bring himself to include another woman in his life on more than a strictly platonic basis.

Panopoulos was a guest at the wedding tomorrow.

Walking through to the kitchen, he tossed the paper into the trash. His jaw tightened at the thought that he would have fend off the Greek, as well.

He guessed he should be glad that it was Zane Carla seemed to be attracted to and not Panopoulos.

Zane had been controllable, so far. And if he stepped over the line, there was always the option that they could settle the issue in the old-fashioned way, down on the beach and without an audience.

Dinner passed in a polite, superficial haze. Carla made conversation, smiled on cue, and avoided looking at Lucas. Unfortunately, because he was seated almost directly opposite her, she was burningly aware of him through each course.

Dessert was served. Still caught between the raw misery that threatened to drag her under, and the need to maintain the appearance of normality, Carla ate. She had reached the dessert course when she registered how much wine she had drunk.

A small sharp shock went through her. She wasn't drunk, but alcohol and some of the foods she was eating did not mix happily with an ulcer. Strictly speaking, after the episode with the virus and the ulcer, she wasn't supposed to drink at all.

Setting her spoon down, she picked up her clutch and excused herself from the table. She asked one of the waitstaff to direct her to the nearest bathroom. Unfortunately, since her grasp of Medinian was far from perfect, she somehow managed to take a wrong turn.

After traversing a long corridor and opening a number of doors, one of which seemed to be the entrance to a private set of rooms, complete with a kitchenette, she opened a door and found herself on a terrace overlooking the sea. Shrugging, because the terrace would do as well as a bathroom since all she required was privacy to take the small cocktail of pills her doctor had prescribed, she walked to the stone parapet and studied the view.

The stiff sea breeze that had been blowing earlier had dropped away, leaving the night still, the air balmy and heavily scented with the pine and rosemary that grew wild on the hills. A huge full moon glowed a rich, buttery gold on the horizon.

Setting her handbag down on the stone pavers, she extracted the MediPACK of pills she had brought with her, tore open the plastic seal and swallowed them dry.

Dropping the plastic waste into her handbag, she straightened just as the door onto the terrace popped open. Her chest tightened when she recognized Lucas.

"I hope you weren't expecting Zane?"

"If I was, it wouldn't be any of your business."

"Zane won't give you what you want."

Carla swallowed to try and clear the dry bitterness in her

mouth. "A loving relationship? The kind of relationship I thought we could have had?"

He ignored the questions. "You should return to the dining room."

The flatness of Lucas's voice startled her. Lucas had always been exciting and difficult to pin down, but he had also been funny and unexpectedly tender. This was the first time she had ever seen this side of him. "Not yet. I have a…headache, I need some air." Which was no lie, because the headache was there, throbbing steadily at her temples.

She pretended to be absorbed by the spectacular view of the crystal-clear night and the vast expanse of sea gleaming like polished bronze beneath the moon. Just off the coast of Medinos, the island of Ambrus loomed, tonight seemingly almost close enough to touch. One of the more substantial islands in the Medinos group, Ambrus was intimately familiar to her because her family had once owned a chunk of it.

"How did you know these are my rooms?"

She spun, shocked at Lucas's closeness and what he'd just said. "I didn't. I was looking for a bathroom. I must have taken a wrong turn."

The coolness of his glance informed her that he didn't quite believe her. Any idea that Lucas would tell her that he had made a mistake and that he desperately wanted her back died a quick death.

A throb of grief hit her at the animosity that seemed to be growing by the second and she pulled herself up sharply. She had run the gamut of shock and anger. She was not going to wallow in self-pity.

It was clear Lucas wasn't going to leave until she did, so she picked up her bag and started toward the door.

Instead of moving aside, Lucas moved to block her path. "I'm sorry you found out this way. I did try to meet with you before dinner."

Her heart suddenly pounding off the register, she stared rigidly at his shoulder. "You could have told me when I called to cancel and given me some time. Even a text would have helped."

His dark brows jerked together. "I'm not in the habit of breaking off relationships over the phone or by text. I wanted to tell you face-to-face."

Her jaw tightened. It didn't help that his gaze was direct, that he was clearly intent on softening the blow. The last thing she wanted from Lucas was pity. "Did Lilah fly in with you?"

"She arrived this afternoon."

Relief made her feel faintly unsteady. So, Lilah hadn't been with Lucas in the limousine.

As insignificant as that detail was, it mattered, because when she had seen the limousine she had been crazily, sappily fantasizing about Lucas and the life they could now share. Although she should have known he hadn't arrived with Lilah, because there hadn't been any media reports that he had arrived at the airport with a female companion.

Lucas's gaze connected with hers. "Before you go back inside, I need to know if you intend to go to the press with a story about our affair."

Affair.

Her chin jerked up. For two years she had considered they had been involved in a relationship. "I'm here for Sienna's wedding. It's her day, and I don't intend to spoil it."

"Good. Because if you try to force my hand by going public with this, take it from me, I'm not playing."

Comprehension hit. She had been so absorbed with the publicity for Ambrosi's latest collection and the crazy rush to organize Sienna's wedding that she had barely had time to sleep, let alone think. When Sienna married Constantine, Carla would be inextricably bound to the Atraeus family.

The Atraeus family were traditionalists. If it were discovered that she and Lucas had been seeing each other secretly for two years, he would come under intense pressure from his family to marry her.

Now the comment about her looking for his rooms made sense.

What better way to force a commitment than to arrange for them both to be found together in his rooms at the *castello?* Anger and a burning sense of shame that he should think she would stoop that low sliced through her. "I hadn't considered that angle."

Why would she when she had assumed Lucas wanted her?

He ignored her statement. "If it's marriage you want, you won't get it by pressuring me."

Which meant he really had thought about the different ways she could force him to the altar. She took a deep breath against a sharp spasm of hurt. "At what point did I ever say I was after marriage?"

His gaze bored into hers, as fierce and obdurate as the dark stone from which the fortress was built. "Then we have an understanding?"

"Oh, I think so." She forced a bright smile. "I wouldn't marry you if you tied me up and dragged me down the aisle. Tell me," she said before she could gag her mouth and instruct her brain to never utter anything that would inform Lucas just how weak and vulnerable she really was. "Did you ever come close to loving me?"

He went still. "What we had wasn't exactly about love."

No. Silly her.

"There's something else we need to talk about."

"In that case, it'll have to wait. Now I really do have a headache." She fumbled in her clutch, searching for the painkillers she'd slipped in before she'd left the villa, just in case. In her haste the foil pack slipped out of her fingers and dropped to the terrace.

Lucas retrieved the pills before she could. "What are these?"

He held the foil pack out of her reach while he read the label. "Since when have you suffered from headaches?"

She snatched the pills from his grasp. "They're a left-over from the virus I caught in Thailand. I don't get them very often."

She ripped the foil open and swallowed two pills dry, grimacing at the extra wave of bitterness in her mouth when one of the pills lodged in her throat. She badly needed a glass of water.

Lucas frowned. "I didn't know you were still having problems."

She shoved the foil pack back in her clutch. "But then you never bothered to ask."

And the last thing she had wanted to do was let him know that she had been so stressed by the unresolved nature of their relationship that she had given herself an even worse stomach ulcer than she had started with two years ago.

After the growing distance between them in Thailand, she hadn't wanted to further undermine their relationship or give him an excuse to break up with her. Keeping silent had been a constant strain because she had wanted the comfort of his presence, had *needed* him near, but now she was glad she hadn't revealed how sick she really had been. It was one small corner of her life that he hadn't invaded, one small batch of memories that didn't contain him.

She felt like kicking herself for being so stupid over the past couple of months. If Lucas had wanted to be with her he would have arranged time together. Once, he had flown into Sydney with only a four-hour window before he'd had to fly out again. They had spent every available second of those four hours locked together in bed.

Cold settled in her stomach. In retrospect, their relationship had foundered in Thailand. Lucas hadn't liked crossing the line into caring; he had simply wanted a pretty, adoring lover and uncomplicated sex.

Lucas was still blocking her path. "You're pale and your eyes are dilated. I'll take you home."

"No." She stepped neatly around him and made a beeline for the open door. Her heart sped up when she realized he was close behind her. "I can drive myself. The last thing I want is to spend any more time with you."

"Too bad." His hand curled around her upper arm, sending a hot, tingling shock straight to the pit of her stomach as he propelled her into the hall. "You've had a couple of glasses of wine, and now a strong painkiller. The last thing you should do is get behind the wheel of that little sports car."

She shot him a coolly assessing look. "Or talk to the paparazzi at the gate."

"Right now it's the hairpin bends on the road back to the villa that worry me."

Something snapped inside her at the calm, matter-of-fact tone of his voice, as if he was conducting damage control in one of his business takeovers. "What do you think I'm going to do, Lucas? Drive off one of your cliffs into the sea?"

Unexpectedly his grip loosened. Twisting free, she grasped the handle of the door to the suite she had briefly checked out before, thinking it could be a bathroom. It was Lucas's suite, apparently. Forbidden territory.

Flinging the door wide, she stepped inside. She was about to prove that at least one of Lucas's fears was justified.

She was going to be her control-freak, ticked-off, stressed-out self for just a few minutes.

She was going to behave badly.

Four

The paralyzing fear that had gripped Lucas at the thought of Carla driving her sports car on Medinos's narrow roads turned to frustration as she stepped inside his suite.

Grimly, he wondered what had happened to the dominance and control with which he had started the evening.

Across boardroom tables, he was aware that his very presence often inspired actual fear. His own people jumped to do his bidding.

Unfortunately, when it came to Carla Ambrosi, concepts like power, control and discipline crashed and burned.

He closed the door behind him. "What do you think you're doing?"

Carla halted by an ebony cabinet that held a selection of bottles, a jug of ice water and a tray of glasses. "I need a drink."

Glass clinked on glass, liquid splashed. His frustration deepened. Carla seldom drank and when she did it had always been in moderation. Tonight he knew she'd had champagne, then wine with dinner. He had kept a watch on her intake, specifically so he could intervene if he thought she was in danger of drinking too much then making a scene. He had been looking for an opportunity to speak to her alone when she had walked out halfway through dessert. Until now he had been certain she wasn't drunk.

He reached her in two long strides and gripped her wrist. "How much have you had?"

Liquid splashed the front of her dress. He jerked his gaze away from the way the wet silk clung to the curve of her breasts.

Her gaze narrowed. A split second later cold liquid cascaded down his chest, soaking through to the skin.

Water, not alcohol.

Time seemed to slow, stop as he stared at her narrowed gaze, delicately molded cheekbones and firm jaw, the rapid pulse at her throat.

The thud of the glass hitting the thick kilim barely registered as she curled her fingers in the lapel of his jacket.

"What do you think you're doing?" His voice was husky, the question automatic as he stared at her face.

"Conducting an experiment."

Her arms slid around his neck; she lifted up onto her toes. Automatically, his head bent. The second his mouth touched hers he knew it was a mistake. Relief shuddered through him as her breasts flattened against his chest and the soft curve of her abdomen cradled his instant arousal.

His hands settled at her waist as he deepened the kiss. The soft, exotic perfume she wore rose up, beguiling him, and the fierce clamp of desire intensified. Two months. As intent as he had been on finishing with Carla, he didn't know how he had stayed away.

No one else did this to him; no one came close. To say he

made love with Carla didn't cover the fierceness of his need or the undisciplined emotion that grabbed at him every time he weakened and allowed himself the "fix" of a small window of time in her bed.

Following the tragedy with Sophie, he had kept his liaisons clear-cut and controlled, as disciplined as his heavy work schedule and workout routines. He had been too shell-shocked to do anything else. Carla was the antithesis of the sophisticated, emotionally secure women he usually chose. Women who didn't demand or do anything flamboyant or off-the-wall.

He dragged his mouth free, shrugged out of his jacket then sank back into the softness of her mouth. He felt her fingers dragging at the buttons of his shirt, the tactile pleasure of her palms sliding over his skin.

Long, drugging minutes passed as he simply kissed her, relearning her touch, her taste. When she moved restlessly against him, he smoothed his hands up over her back, knowing instinctively that if she was going to withdraw, this would be the moment.

Her gaze clashed with his and he logged her assent. It occurred to Lucas that if he had been a true gentleman, he would have eased away, slowed things down. Instead he gave into temptation, cupped her breasts through the flimsy silk of bodice and bra. She arched against him with a small cry. Heat jerked through him when he realized she had climaxed.

Every muscle taut, he swept her into his arms and carried her to the couch. Her arms wound around his neck as she pulled him down with her. At some point his shirt disappeared and Carla shimmied against him, lifting up the few centimeters he needed so he could peel away the flimsy scrap of silk and lace that served as underwear.

He felt her fingers tearing at the fastening of his trousers. In some distant part of his mind the fact that he didn't have a condom registered. A split second later her hands closed around him and he ceased to think.

Desire shivered and burned through Carla as Lucas's hands framed her hips. Still dazed by the unexpected power of her climax, she automatically tilted her hips, allowing him access. Shock reverberated through her when she registered that there was no condom.

She hadn't thought; he hadn't asked. In retrospect she hadn't wanted to ask. She had been drowning in sensation, caught and held by the sudden powerful conviction that if she walked away from Lucas now, everything they had shared, everything they had been to each other would be lost. She would never touch him, kiss him, make love with him again, and that thought was acutely painful.

It was wrong, crazily wrong, on a whole lot of levels. Lucas had broken up with her. He had chosen someone else.

His gaze locked with hers and the steady, focused heat, so utterly familiar—as if she really was the only woman in the world for him—steadied her.

Emotion squeezed her chest as the shattering intensity gripped her again, linking her more intensely with Lucas. She should pull back, disengage. Making love did not compute, and especially not without a condom, but the concept of stopping now was growing progressively more blurred and distant.

She didn't want distance. She loved making love with Lucas. She loved his scent, the satiny texture of skin, the masculine beauty of sleek, hard muscle. The tender way he touched her, kissed her, made love to her was indescribably singular and intimate. She had never made love with another man, and when they were together, for those moments, he was *hers*.

Sharp awareness flickered in his gaze. He muttered something in rapid, husky Medinian, an apology for his loss of control, and a wild sliver of hope made her tense. If Lucas had wanted her badly enough that he hadn't been able to stop long enough to take care of protection, then there had to be a future for them.

With a raw groan he tangled his fingers in her hair, a glint of rueful humor charming her as he bent and softly kissed her. Something small and hurt inside her relaxed. She wound her arms around his neck, holding him tight against her and the hot night shivered and dissolved around them.

For long minutes Carla lay locked beneath Lucas on the couch. She registered the warm internal tingle of lovemaking. It had been two months since they had last been together, and she took a moment to wallow in the sheer pleasure of his heat and scent, the uncomplicated sensuality of his weight pressing her down.

She rubbed her palms down his back and felt his instant response.

Lucas's head lifted up from its resting place on her shoulder. The abrupt wariness in his gaze reflected her own thoughts. They'd had unprotected sex once. Were they really going to repeat the mistake?

A sharp rap at the door completed the moment of separation.

"Wait," Lucas said softly.

She felt the cool flutter as he draped her dress over her thighs. Feeling dazed and guilty, Carla clambered to her feet, snatched up her panties and her bag and found her shoes.

"The bathroom is the second on the left."

Her head jerked up at the husky note in his voice, but Lucas's expression was back to closed, his gaze neutral.

He was already dressed. With his shirt buttoned, his jacket on, he looked smoothly powerful and unruffled, exactly as he had before they had made love. Somewhere inside her the sliver of hope that had flared to life when they had been making love died a sudden death.

Nothing had changed. How many times had she seen him distance himself from her in just that way when he had left her apartment, as if he had already separated himself from her emotionally?

As if what they had shared was already filed firmly in the past and she had no place in his everyday life.

The moment was chilling, a reality check that was long overdue. "Don't worry, I'll find it. I don't want anyone to know I was here, either." Her own voice was husky but steady. Despite the hurt she felt oddly distant and remote.

She stepped into the cool, tiled sanctuary of the bathroom and locked the door. After freshening up she set about fixing her makeup. A sharp rap on the door made her jerk, smearing her mascara.

"When you're ready, I'll take you home."

"Five minutes. And I'll take myself home."

She stared at her reflection, her too pale skin, the curious blankness in her eyes as if, like a turtle retreating into its shell, the hurt inner part of her had already withdrawn. With automatic movements, she cleaned away the smear and reapplied the mascara.

When she stepped out of the bathroom the sitting room was empty. For the first time she noticed the fine antiques and jewel-bright rugs, the art that decorated the walls and which was lit by glowing pools of light.

Lucas stepped in from the terrace, through an elegant set of French doors.

She met his gaze squarely. "Who was at the door?"

"Lilah."

Oh, good. Her life had just officially gone to hell in a handbasket. "Did she see me?"

"Unfortunately."

Lucas's choice of word finally succeeded in dissolving the curious blankness and suddenly she was fiercely angry. "What if I'm pregnant?"

A pulse worked in his jaw. "If you're pregnant, that changes things—we'll talk. Until you have confirmation, we forget this happened."

When Carla woke in the morning, the headache was still nagging, and she was definitely off-color. She stepped into the shower and washed her hair. When she'd soaped herself, she stood beneath the stream of hot water and waited to feel better.

She spread her palm over her flat abdomen, a sense of disorientation gripping her when she considered that she could be pregnant.

A baby.

The thought was as shocking as the fact that she had been weak enough to allow Lucas to make love to her.

If she was pregnant, she decided, there was no way she could terminate. She loved babies, the way they smelled, their downy softness and vulnerability, the gummy smiles— and she would adore her own.

Decision made. If—and it was a big *if*—she was pregnant she would have the child and manage as a single parent. Lucas wouldn't have to be involved. There was no way she would marry him without love, or exist in some kind of twilight state in his life that would allow him discreet access while he married someone else.

Turning off the water, she toweled herself dry, belted on a robe and padded down to breakfast. Her stomach felt vaguely nauseous and she wasn't hungry, but she forced herself to chew one of the sweet Medinian rolls she had enjoyed so much yesterday.

Half an hour later, she checked on Sienna, who was

smothered by attendants, then dressed for the wedding in an exquisite lilac-silk sheath. She sat for the hairdresser, who turned her hair into a glossy confection of curls piled on top of her head, then moved to another room where a cosmetician chatted cheerfully while she did her makeup.

Several hours later, with the wedding formalities finally completed and the dancing under way, she was finally free to leave her seat at the bridal table. Technically, as the maid of honor, her partner for the celebration was Lucas, who was the best man. Mercifully, he was seated to one side of the bride and groom, and she the other, so she had barely seen him all evening.

As she rose from the table and found the strap of her purse, which was looped over the back of her seat, lean brown fingers closed over hers, preventing her from lifting up the bag.

A short, sharp shock ran through her at the pressure. Lucas released his hold on her fingers almost immediately.

He indicated Constantine and Sienna drifting around the dance floor. "I know you probably don't want to dance, but tradition demands that we take the floor next."

She glanced away from the taut planes of his cheekbones and his chiseled jaw, the inky crescents of his lashes. In a morning suit, with its tight waistcoat, he looked even more devastatingly handsome than usual. "And is that what you do?" she said a little bitterly. "Follow tradition?"

Lucas waited patiently for her to acquiesce to the dance. "You know me better than that."

Yes, she did, unfortunately. As wealthy and privileged as Lucas was, he had done a number of unconventional things. One of them was to play professional rugby. Her gaze rested on the faintly battered line of his nose. An automatic tingle of awareness shot through her at the dangerous, sexy edge it added to features that would otherwise have been *GQ* perfect.

His gaze locked on hers and, as suddenly as if a switch had been thrown, the sizzling hum of attraction was intimately, crazily shared.

Her breath came in sharply. Not good.

Aware that they were now under intense scrutiny from guests at a nearby table, including Lilah, Carla placed her hand on Lucas's arm and allowed him to lead her to the dance floor.

Lucas's breath feathered her cheek as he pulled her close. "How likely is it that you are pregnant?"

She stiffened at the sudden hot flood of memory. On cue the music changed, slowing to a sultry waltz. Lucas pulled her into a closer hold. Heat shivered through her as her body automatically responded to his touch. "Not likely."

Since the virus she had caught in Thailand she hadn't had a regular cycle, mostly because, initially, she had lost so much weight. She had regained some of the weight but she hadn't yet had a period. Although she wasn't about to inform Lucas of that fact.

"How soon will you know?"

"I'm not sure. Two weeks, give or take."

"When you find out, one way or the other, I want to be informed, but that shouldn't be a problem. As of next week, I'm Ambrosi's new CEO."

She stumbled, missing a step. Lucas's arm tightened and she found herself briefly pressed against his muscular frame. Jerkily, she straightened, her cheeks burning at the intimate brush of his hips, a stark reminder of their lovemaking last night. "I thought Ben Vitalis was stepping in as CEO."

Lucas's specialty was managing hostile acquisitions. Since her family, embattled by long-term debt, had voluntarily offered The Atraeus Group a majority shareholding of Ambrosi Pearls, the situation was cut-and-dried. Lucas shouldn't have come within a mile of Ambrosi.

Unless he viewed *her* as a problem.

Her chin jerked up as another thought occurred to her. "You told Constantine about us."

His brows jerked together. "No."

Relief flooded her. The thought that Lucas could have revealed their relationship now, when it was over, would have finally succeeded in making her feel cheap and disposable.

She drew in a steadying breath. "When was the decision made?"

"A few weeks ago, when we knew Ambrosi was in trouble."

"It's not necessary for you to come to Sydney. In the unlikely event that there is a baby, I will contact you."

His glance was impatient. "The decision is made."

She drew an impeded breath at the sudden graphic image of herself round and heavy with his child. She didn't think a pregnancy was possible, but clearly Lucas did.

The music wound to a sweeping, romantic halt. There was a smattering of applause. Carla allowed Lucas to complete the formalities by leading her off the dance floor.

The rest of the evening passed in a haze. Carla danced with several men she didn't know, and twice with Alex Panopoulos, an Ambrosi client she'd had extensive dealings with in Sydney. The wealthy owner of a successful chain of high-end retail stores, Alex was a reptile when it came to women. He was also in need of a public relations officer for a new venture and spent the first dance fishing to see if she was available. Halfway through the second dance, Lucas cut in.

His gaze clashed with hers as he spun her into a sweeping turn. "Damn. What are you doing with Panopoulos?"

"Nothing that's any of your business. Why? Do you think

I'm in danger of meeting a man who might actually propose?"

"Alex Panopoulos is a shrewd operator. When he marries, there will be a business connection."

She stared at the clean line of his jaw. "Are you suggesting that all he wants is an affair?"

His grip on her fingers tightened. "I have no idea what Panopoulos wants. All I know is that when it comes to women he doesn't have a very savory reputation."

"I'm surprised you think I need protection."

"Trust me, you don't want to get involved with Panopoulos."

Dragging free of his gaze, she stared at the muscular column of his throat. "Maybe he wanted something from me that has nothing to do with sex? Besides, you're wasting your breath trying to protect me. From now on, who I choose to be with is none of your business."

"It is if you're pregnant."

The flash of possessive heat in his gaze and the tightening of his hold finally succeeded in making her lose her temper. "I might have some say in that."

Five

Lucas leaned against the wall in a dim alcove, arms folded over his chest as he observed the final formality of the wedding, the throwing of the bouquet.

Zane joined him, shifting through the shadows with the fluid ease that was more a by-product of his time spent on the streets of L.A. than of the strict, conventional upbringing he'd received on Medinos. He nodded at Carla, who was part of a cluster of young women gathered on the dance floor. "Not your finest hour. But, if you hadn't rescued her, I was thinking of doing it myself."

"Touch Carla," Lucas said softly, "and you lose your hand."

Zane took a swallow of beer. "Thought so."

Lucas eyed his younger brother with irritation. Four years difference and he felt like Methuselah. "How long have you known?"

"About a year, give or take."

The bouquet arced through the air straight into Carla's hands. Lucas's jaw tightened as she briskly handed it to one of the pretty young flower girls and detached herself from the noisy group. She made a beeline for her table, picked up the lilac clutch that went with her dress, and made her way out of the *castello's* ballroom.

Lucas glanced at Zane. "Do me a favor and look after Lilah for me for the rest of the evening."

Zane's expression registered rare startlement. "Let me get this right, you won't let me near Carla, but with Lilah it's okay?"

Lucas frowned at his turn of phrase, but his attention was focused on the elegant line of Carla's back. "The party's almost over. An hour, max."

"That long."

Impatiently, he studied the now empty hallway. "She'll need a ride back to the villa."

"Not a problem. Aunts at six o'clock." With a jerk of his chin, indicating direction, Zane snagged his beer and made a swift exit.

Pushing away from the wall, Lucas started after Carla, and found himself the recipient of a shrewd glance from his mother and steely speculation from a gaggle of silver-haired great-aunts.

He groaned inwardly, annoyed that he had dropped his guard enough that not only Zane but his mother had become aware of his interest in Carla. The last thing he needed was his mother interfering in his love life.

Seconds later, he traversed the vaulted hallway and stepped outside onto the graveled driveway just as the sound of Constantine and Sienna's departing helicopter cut the air.

The sun was gone, the night thick with stars, but heat still flowed out of the sunbaked soil as he strode toward Carla.

The ambient temperature was still hot enough that he felt uncomfortable in his suit jacket.

A stiff sea breeze was blowing, tugging strands loose from the rich, dark coils piled on top of Carla's head, making her look sexily disheveled. The breeze also plastered her dress against her body, emphasizing just how much weight she had lost.

His frown deepened. A regular gym bunny, Carla had always been fit and toned, with firm but definite curves. The curves were still there but if he didn't miss his guess she had dropped at least a dress size. After the virus she had picked up in Thailand, weight loss was understandable, but she should have regained it by now.

She spun when she heard the crunch of gravel beneath his shoes. A small jolt went through him when he registered the blankness of her gaze.

Carla didn't do sad. She had always been confident, sassy and adept at using her feminine power to the max. For Carla, masculine conquest was as natural as breathing. He had assumed that when their relationship was at an end she would have a lineup of prospective boyfriends eager to fill the gap.

In that moment it hit him forcibly that as similar as Carla was to Sophie with her job and her lifestyle, there were some differences. Sophie had been immature and self-centered, while Carla was fiercely loyal to her sister and her family, to the point of putting her own needs aside so as not to hurt Sienna. Even though that loyalty had clashed with what he had wanted, he had respected it. It also occurred to him that in her own way, Carla had been fiercely loyal to him. She had dated other men, but only ever in a business context for Ambrosi Pearls.

Broodingly, he considered the fact that Carla had been a virgin the first time they had made love, that she had never slept with anyone but him. He realized he had conveniently pushed the knowledge aside because it hadn't fitted the picture of Carla he had wanted to see.

He had been the one who had held back and played it safe, not Carla, and now the sheer intimacy of their situation kept hitting him like a kick to the chest.

He should let her go, but the shattering fact that he could have made her pregnant had changed something vital in his hard drive.

They were linked, at least until he had ascertained whether or not she was carrying his child. Despite his need to end the relationship, he couldn't help but feel relieved about that fact. "The limousines are gone. If you want a lift, I'll drive you."

"That won't be necessary." Carla extracted a cell phone from her clutch. "I'll get a taxi."

"Unless you've prebooked, with all the guests on Medinos for the wedding, you'll have difficulty getting one tonight."

She frowned as she flipped the phone closed and slipped it back in her clutch. "Then I'll ask Constantine."

He jerked his head in the direction of the helicopter, which was rapidly turning into a small dot on the horizon. "Constantine is on honeymoon. I'll take you."

Her glare was pointed. "I don't understand what you're doing out here. Shouldn't you be looking after your new girlfriend?"

"Zane's taking care of Lilah." Before she could argue, he cupped her elbow and steered her in the direction of the *castello's* stable of garages.

She jerked free of his hold. "Why doesn't Zane take me home and you go and take care of Lilah?"

His jaw clamped. "Do you want the lift or not?"

She stared at a point somewhere just left of his shoulder. Enough time passed that his temper began to spiral out of control.

Carla shrugged. "I'll accept a lift because I need one, but please don't touch me again."

"I wasn't trying to 'touch' you."

Her gaze connected with his, shooting blue fire. "I know what you were doing. The same thing you tried to do on the dance floor. Save it for Lilah."

He suppressed the cavemanlike urge to simply pick her up and carry her to the car. "You don't look well. What's wrong with you?"

"Nothing that a good night's sleep won't fix." Her gaze narrowed. "Why don't you say what's really bothering you? That, with all the paparazzi still on the loose, you can't take the risk that I might give them a story? And I think we both know that I could give them quite a story, an exposé of the *real* Lucas—"

Lucas gave in to the caveman urge and picked her up. "Did I mention the paparazzi?"

She thumped his shoulder with her beaded purse. "Let me down!"

Obligingly, he set her down by the passenger door of the Maserati. He jerked the door open. "Get in. If you try to run I'll come after you."

"There has to be a law against this." But she climbed into the sleek leather bucket seat.

"On Medinos?" Despite his temper, Lucas's mouth twitched as he slid behind the wheel and turned the key in the ignition. For the first time in two months he felt oddly content. "Not for an Atraeus."

Carla's tension skyrocketed when, instead of responding to her request and parking out on the street, Lucas drove into the cobbled driveway of the villa. At that point, he insisted on taking the house key from her and unlocked the door. When she attempted to close the door on him, he simply stepped past her and walked into the small, elegant house, switching on lights.

A narky little tension headache throbbing at her temples, Carla made a beeline for the bathroom, filled the glass on the counter with water and took her pills. Refilling the glass, she sat down on the edge of the bath and sipped, waiting to feel better.

A sharp rap on the bathroom door made her temper soar. She had hoped Lucas would take the hint and leave, but apparently he was still in the house. Replacing the glass on the counter, she checked her appearance then unlocked the door and stepped out into the hall.

He was leaning against the wall, arms crossed over his chest. She tried not to notice that, though he was still wearing his jacket, his tie and waistcoat were gone and several buttons of his shirt were undone revealing a mouthwatering slice of bronzed skin. "I'm fine now. You can leave."

She stepped past him and headed for the front door. Her spine tightened as Lucas followed too close behind, and she remembered what had happened the last time they had been alone together.

Note to self, she thought grimly as he peeled off into the sitting room and picked up his tie and waistcoat, *do not allow yourself to be alone with Lucas again.*

Opening the front door, she stood to one side, allowing him plenty of space. "Thank you for the lift."

He paused at the open door, making her aware of his height, the width of his shoulders, the power and vitality that seemed to burn from him. "Maybe you should see a doctor."

"If I need medical help, I'll get it for myself." She glanced pointedly at her wristwatch, resisting the urge to squint because one of the annoying symptoms of the headache now seemed to be that her eyes were ultrasensitive to light.

Not good. Her doctor had warned her that stress could

cause a viral relapse. With her father's funeral, Sienna's wedding and the breakup with Lucas, she was most definitely under stress.

His hand landed on the wall beside her head. Suddenly he was close enough that his heat engulfed her, and his clean, faintly exotic scent filled her nostrils.

Grimly, she resisted the impulse to take the half step needed, wrap her arms around his neck and melt into a goodnight kiss that would very likely turn into something else. "Um, shouldn't you be getting back to Lilah?"

For the briefest of moments he hesitated. His gaze dropped to her mouth and despite the tiredness that pulled at her, she found herself holding her breath, awareness humming through every cell of her being.

He let out a breath. "We can't do this again."

"No." But it had been an effort to say that one little word, and humiliation burned through her that, despite everything, she was still weak enough to want him.

His hand closed into a fist beside her head, then he was gone, the door closing gently behind him.

Carla leaned her forehead against the cool cedar of the door, her face burning.

Darn, darn, darn. Why had she almost given in to him? Like a mindless, trained automaton responding to the merest suggestion that he might kiss her.

After the stern talking-to she had given herself following the episode on the dance floor, she had succeeded in making herself look needy, like a woman who would do anything to get him back into her bed.

The pressure at her temples sharpened. Feeling more unsteady by the second, as if she was coming down with the flu, Carla walked to her bedroom. The acute sensitivity of her eyes was making it difficult to stand being in a lit room. No doubt about it, the virus had taken hold.

Removing her jewelry, she changed into cool cotton drawstring pants and a tank. She pulled on a cotton sweatshirt and cozy slippers against the chill and walked through to the bathroom. After washing and moisturizing her face, she pulled the pins out of her hair, which was an instant relief.

A discreet vibration made her frown. Her cell phone had a musical ring tone, and so did Sienna's. Margaret Ambrosi didn't own a cell, which meant the phone must belong to Lucas.

She padded barefoot into the sitting room in time to see the phone vibrate itself off the coffee table and drop to the carpet. A small pinging sound followed.

Carla picked up the phone. Lucas had missed a call from Lilah; now he had a text message, also from Lilah.

Fingers shaking slightly, she attempted to read the text but was locked out. A message popped up requesting she unlock the phone.

Not a problem, unless Lucas had changed his PIN since the last time they had dated.

Not dated, she corrected, her mood taking another dive. *Slept together.*

The last time he had stayed over at her apartment, before the holiday in Thailand, Lucas had needed to buy a new phone. The PIN he had used had been her birth date. At the time she had been ridiculously happy at his sentimental streak. She had taken it as a definite, positive *sign* that their relationship was progressing in the right direction.

She held her breath as she keyed in the number. The mail menu opened up.

The message was simple and to the point. Lilah was waiting for Lucas to call and would stay up until she heard from him.

The sick feeling in her stomach, the prickling chill she'd felt when he had broken up with her the previous night, came back at her full force. If she'd needed reinforcement of her decision to stay clear of Lucas Atraeus, this was it.

He was involved with someone else. He had *chosen* someone else, and the new woman in his life was waiting for him.

Closing the message, she replaced the phone on the coffee table and walked back to the bathroom. She switched off lights as she went, leaving one lamp burning in the sitting room for her mother when she came home. The relief of semidarkness was immense.

In the space of the past few minutes, she realized, the throbbing in her head had intensified and her skin hurt to touch. She swallowed another headache tablet, washing it down with sips of water. The sound of the doorbell jerked her head up. The sharp movement sent a stab of hot pain through her skull.

Lucas, back for his phone.

Setting the glass down, she walked back out to the hall, which was lit by the glow from the porch light streaming through two frosted sidelight windows. The buzzer sounded again.

"Open up, Carla. All I want is my phone."

That particular request, she decided, was the equivalent of waving a red rag at a bull. "You can have the phone tomorrow."

"I still have the key to this door," he said quietly. "If you don't unlock it, I'll let myself in."

Over her dead body.

"Just a minute." Annoyed with herself for forgetting to reclaim the key, she reached for the chain and tried to engage it. In her haste it slipped from her fingers.

She heard Lucas say something short and sharp. Adrenaline pumped. He knew she was trying to chain the door against him. The metallic scrape of a key being inserted into the lock was preternaturally loud as she grabbed the chain again.

Before she could slot it into place the door swung open, pushing her back a half step. Normally, the half step back wouldn't have fazed her, but with the weird shakiness of the virus she was definitely not her normal, athletic self and had to clutch at the hall table to help with her balance. Something crashed to the floor; glass shattered. She registered that when she had grabbed at the table her shoulder must have brushed against a framed watercolor mounted on the wall.

Lucas frowned. "Don't move."

Ignoring him, she bent down and grasped the edge of the frame.

Lean fingers curled around her upper arms, hauling her upright. "Leave that. You'll cut yourself."

Too late. Curling her thumb in against her palm, she made a fist, hiding a tiny, stinging jab that as far as she was concerned was so small it didn't count as a cut. She blinked at the bright porch light. "I didn't give you permission to come in, and you don't have the right to give me orders."

"You *did* cut yourself." He muttered something in Medinian. She was pretty sure it was a curse word. "Give me the watercolor before you do any more damage."

Her grip on the watercolor firmed, even though his request made sense. If she got blood on the painting it would be ruined. "I don't need your help. Get your phone and go."

"You look terrible."

"Thanks!"

"You're as white as a sheet."

He released her so suddenly she swayed off balance. By the time she recovered he had laid claim to her sore thumb and was probing at the small cut. But she still had the painting. "Neat trick."

His gaze was oddly intent. "There doesn't seem to be any glass in it."

He wrapped a handkerchief around her thumb and closed her fingers around it to apply pressure. "How long have you been sick?"

Her jaw tightened. She was being childish, she knew, but she hated being sick. It literally brought out the worst in her. "I'm not sick. Like I said before, all I need is a good night's sleep, so if you don't mind—"

The brush of his fingers against her temple as he pushed hair away from her face distracted her.

"Does that hurt? Don't answer. I can see that it does."

He leaned close. Arrested by his nearness, she studied the taut line of his jaw, suddenly assaulted by a myriad of sensations—the heat from Lucas's body, the clean scent of his skin, the rasp of his indrawn breath. That was one of the weird things about the virus: it seemed to amplify everything, hearing, scent, emotions, as if protective layers had been peeled away, leaving her senses bare and open.

In a slick move, he took the watercolor while her attention was occupied by the intriguing shape of his cheekbones, which were meltdown material.

A small sound informed her that he had placed the painting on the hall table. Out of nowhere her stomach turned an uncomfortable somersault. "I think I'm going to be sick."

His hand closed around her upper arm, and the heat from his palm burned through the cotton sweatshirt. Then they were moving, glass crunching under the soles of her slippers as he guided her out of the entrance hall into the sitting room. Another turn and they were in the bathroom.

Long minutes later, she rinsed her mouth and washed her face. She had hoped that Lucas would have left, but he was leaning against the hallway wall looking patient and com-

posed and drop-dead gorgeous. In contrast she felt bedraggled and washed-out and as limp as a noodle.

Disgust and a taut, burning humiliation filled her. It was a rerun of Thailand, everything she had never wanted to happen again.

He folded his arms across his chest. "I'm guessing this is a relapse of the virus."

Keeping one hand on the wall for steadiness, she made a beeline for her bedroom. "Apparently. This is the first recurrence I've had." Her head spun and for a split second she thought she might be sick again, although she was fairly certain there was nothing left in her stomach. Two more wavering steps then the blissful darkness of her bedroom enfolded her. "Don't turn on the light. And don't come in here. This is *my* room." And as such it was off-limits to men who didn't love her.

"You should have told me you were still ill."

Her temper flashed, but if it was measured on a color spectrum it would have been a washed-out pink, not the angry red it had been earlier in the evening. She didn't have the energy for anything more and she was fading fast. "I didn't *know* I was still ill."

"That's some temper you've got."

Her teeth would have gritted if she'd had the strength. "Inherited it from my mother." She dragged her coverlet back. "She'll be home soon." The thought filled her with extreme satisfaction. She hadn't been able to kick Lucas's butt out, but Margaret Ambrosi would. Especially if she found him in her little girl's room.

Gingerly she sat on the side of the bed. Now that the stomach issue was over her attention was back on her head, which was pounding. What she needed was another painkiller, because the last one had just been flushed.

Dimly, she registered that despite her express order, Lucas *was* in her room. "I told you not to be here."

He crouched down and eased her slippers off her feet. "Or what? You'll lose that famous temper?"

"That's right." A shiver went through her at the burning heat of his hands on her feet. The chill on her skin made her realize that the next stage of the virus was kicking in. Oh, goody, she thought wearily, Antarctic-cold shivers followed by sweats that rivaled burning desert sands. Exactly how she always wanted to spend a Saturday night.

"I'll take the risk. I survived Thailand, I can survive this."

He pulled her to her feet. Her nose bumped against his shoulder. Automatically, she clutched his lean waist and leaned into his comforting strength. She inhaled, breathing in his scent, and for a crazy moment all she wanted to do was rest there.

A split second later, the sheet peeled back, Lucas eased her into bed and pulled the sheets and coverlet over her.

With a sigh, she allowed her head to sink into the feather pillow. "All I need is another one of the painkillers on the bathroom vanity and some water and I'll be fine." It was surrender, she knew it, but she really did need the pill.

She registered his near silent footfalls as he walked to the bathroom, the hiss of water as he filled the glass, then he was back. His arm came around her shoulders as he propped her up so she could take the pill and drink the water. When she was finished he set the glass down on her bedside table.

She settled back on the pillows. "You know what? You're good at this."

"I had lots of practice in Thailand. Do you need anything else?" His voice was closer now, the timbre low and deliciously gruff.

It was the kind of velvety masculine rumble that, if they had been in bed together, would have invited a snuggling session. Then suddenly she remembered. Lucas was with Lilah now; he no longer wanted her. If he felt anything for her, it had to be pity. A weak, watered-down version of fury roared through her.

She peeled her lids open and peered at Lucas, ready to read him the riot act, then forgot what she was about to say because there was a strange, intent expression on his face. "Nothing. You can leave. Phone's on the coffee table. That was what you came for, wasn't it?"

He was so close she could feel the heat blasting off his body, see his gaze sliding over her features, cataloging her white face and messy hair. For shallow, utterly female reasons she wished that her face was glowing instead of chalky-white and that she had taken the time to brush her hair. Mercifully, the strong painkiller finally kicked in, taking the heat out of the ache in her head and dragging her down into sleep. "I don't want you here."

It was a lie. The virus had made her so weak that she was fast losing the strength to keep up the charade, even to herself.

"I'm staying until I know you'll be all right."

"I would like you to leave. Now." The crisp delivery she intended was spoiled by the fact that the words ran together in a drunken, blurred jumble.

She was certain the soft exhalation she heard had something to do with amusement, which made her even more furious. The mattress shifted as he planted a hand on either side of her head and leaned close. "What are you going to do if I don't? Make me leave?"

For a crazy moment she thought he was actually flirting with her, but that couldn't be. "Don't have to," she mumbled, settling the argument. Her eyelids slid closed. "You've already gone."

Silence settled around her, thick, heavy, as the sedative effect of the pills dragged her down.

"Do you want me back?"

The words jerked her awake, but they had been uttered so quietly she wasn't sure if she had imagined them or if Lucas had actually spoken.

She could see him standing in her bedroom doorway. Maybe she had been dreaming, or worse, hallucinating. "I took codeine, not truth serum."

"It was worth a try."

So he *had* asked the question.

She pushed up on one elbow. The suspicion that he was sneakily trying to interrogate her while she was drowsy from the pills solidified. Although she couldn't fathom why he would be interested in what she really thought and felt now. "I don't know why you're bothering. Thank you for helping me, but please leave now."

He shook his head. "You're…different tonight."

Different? She had been dumped. She had committed the cardinal sin of making love with her ex and could quite possibly be pregnant.

"Not different." Turning over, she punched the pillow and willed herself to go to sleep. "Real."

Six

Ten days later, Carla strolled into the Ambrosi building in Sydney.

When she reached her office, her assistant, Elise, a chirpy blonde with a marketing degree and a formidable memory for names and statistics, was in the process of hanging up the phone. "Lucas wants you in his office. *Now.*"

A jolt of fiery irritation instantly evaporated the peace and calm of four days spent recuperating at her mother's house, the other five in the blissful solitude of the Blue Mountains at a friend's holiday home. "Did he say why?"

Elise looked dreamily reflective. "He's male, hot *and* single. Does it matter?"

Nerves taut, Carla continued on to her desk and deliberately took time out to examine the list of messages and calls Elise had compiled in her absence. Keeping her bag hooked over her shoulder, she checked her calendar and noted she had two meetings scheduled.

When she couldn't stall any longer, she strolled to Sienna's old office, frowning at the changes Atraeus money had already made to her family's faltering business. Worn blue carpet had been replaced with a sleek, dove-gray weave. Fresh paint and strategically placed art now graced walls that had once been decorated solely with monochrome prints of Ambrosi jewelry designs.

Feeling oddly out of place in what, from childhood, had been a cozily familiar setting, she greeted work colleagues.

Directing a brittle smile at Sienna's personal assistant, Nina—Lucas's PA now—she stepped into the elegant corner office.

Lucas, broad shouldered and sleekly powerful in a dark suit with a crisp white shirt and red tie, dominated a room that was still manifestly feminine as he stood at the windows, a phone held to one ear.

His gaze locked with hers, he terminated the call. "Close the door behind you and take a seat."

Suddenly glad she had made an extra effort with her appearance, she closed the door. The sharp little red suit, with its short skirt and fitted V-necked jacket, always made her feel attractive and energized. It probably wasn't the best idea for dealing with Lucas, but she hadn't worn it for him. She had a job interview at five with Alex Panopoulos, and she needed to look confident and professional. His upmarket Pan department stores were branching into jewelry manufacture and he had been chasing her all week to come in for an interview.

She hated the idea of leaving Ambrosi Pearls, but she had to be pragmatic about her position. When Constantine had offered the company back to Sienna on her wedding day they had held a family meeting. In essence, they had agreed to honour their debts, so the transfer of the company to The Atraeus Group had gone through as planned. With Sienna's marriage to Constantine binding both families together, combined with Constantine's assurance that he would keep the company intact, it had seemed the most sensible solution.

As a consequence, Carla now owned a block of voting shares. They would assure her of an income for the rest of her life, but they gave her no effective power. Her current personal contract as Ambrosi Pearls's public relations executive was up for renewal directly after Ambrosi's new product launch in a week's time. She didn't anticipate that Lucas would renew it. Her tenure as "The Face of Ambrosi" was just as shaky, but as she provided that service for free to help the company save money, it was no skin off her nose if Lucas no longer wanted her face on the posters.

Annoyance flickered in Lucas's gaze when she didn't immediately sit. He replaced the phone on its base. "I didn't expect you back in so soon."

She lifted a brow. "I felt okay, so there was no point in staying at home."

"I've been trying to reach you all week. Why didn't you return my calls?"

She shrugged. "I was staying with friends and didn't take my phone." She had left the phone at her apartment on purpose. The last thing she had needed was to have a desperately low moment and make the fatal mistake of trying to call or text Lucas.

There was a small charged silence. "How are you?"

"Fine. A couple of days in bed and the symptoms disappeared." She smiled brightly. "If that's all…"

"Not exactly." His gaze rested on her waist, where the jacket cinched in tight. "Are you pregnant?"

Despite her effort at control, heat flooded her cheeks. "I don't know yet. I have a test kit, but it's early to get an accurate reading."

"When will you know?"

She frowned, feeling distinctly uncomfortable with the subject and the way he was regarding her, as if she was a concubine who had somehow escaped the harem and he had ownership rights. "I should know in another couple of days. But whether I'm pregnant or not, it needn't concern you."

Actually, she could find out right that minute if she wanted. The test kit had said a result could be obtained in as early as seven days. She had studied the instructions then chucked the box in the back of one of her drawers. She still felt too raw and hurt to face using the kit and discovering that not only had she lost Lucas, her life was about to take a huge, unplanned turn. In a few days, when she felt ready, she would do the test.

Anger flickered in his gaze. "You would abort the child?"

"No." She felt shocked that he had even jumped to that conclusion. If there was a child, there was no way she would do anything other than keep the baby and smother it with love for the rest of its life. "What I meant is that *if* there is a child, I've decided that you don't have to worry, because you don't need to be involved, or even acknowledge—"

"Any child of mine would be acknowledged."

The whiplash flatness of his voice, as if she had scraped a raw nerve, was even more shocking. Carla sucked in a breath and forced herself to loosen off the soaring tension. She was clearly missing something here. "This is crazy. I don't know why we're discussing something that might never happen. Is that all you wanted to know?"

"No." He propped himself on the edge of the desk. "Have a seat. There's something else we need to discuss."

There were three comfortable client seats; she chose the one farthest away from Lucas. The second she lowered herself into the chair she regretted the decision. Even though he wasn't standing, Lucas still towered over her. "Let me guess—I'm fired in a week's time? I'm surprised it took you so long to get around to—"

"I'm not firing you."

Carla blinked. Constantine had fired Sienna almost immediately, although his reasons had been understandable. Continuing on as CEO of a company in Sydney while he was based in Medinos had not been viable.

His gaze flicked broodingly over the crisp little suit. "Do you always dress like that for work?"

His sudden change of tack threw her even more off balance. She realized that from his vantage point he could see more than the shadowy hint of cleavage that was normally visible in the vee of the jacket. She squashed the urge to drag the lapels together. "Yes. Is there a problem?"

He crossed his arms over his chest. "Nothing that an extra button or a blouse wouldn't fix."

She shot to her feet. "There is nothing wrong with what I'm wearing. Sienna was perfectly happy with my wardrobe."

He straightened, making her even more aware of his height, the breadth of his shoulders, the incomprehensible anger simmering behind midnight-dark eyes.

"Sienna was female."

"What has that got to do with anything?"

"From where I'm standing, quite a lot.

She didn't know what was bothering him. Maybe a major deal had fallen through, or even better, Lilah had dumped him. Whatever it was she would swear that he was behaving proprietorially, but that couldn't be. He had dumped her without ceremony; he had made it clear he didn't want her. To add insult to injury, the tabloids were having a field day reporting his relationship with Lilah.

His gaze dropped once again to the vee of her jacket. "Who are you meeting today?"

Temper soaring at the lightning perusal, the even more pointed innuendo, she reeled off two names.

"Both male," he said curtly.

"Chandler and Howarth are contemporaries of my father! And I resent the implication that I would resort to using sex to make sales for Ambrosi, but if you prefer I could turn up for work in beige. Or, since this conversation is taking a medieval turn, maybe you'd prefer sackcloth and ashes."

His mouth twitched at the corners and despite her spiraling anger she found herself briefly mesmerized by the sudden jolt of charm. Lucas was handsome when he was cool and ruthless, but when he smiled he was drop-dead gorgeous in a completely masculine way that made her go weak at the knees and melt.

"You don't own anything beige."

"How would you know?" she pointed out, glad to get her teeth into something that could generate some self-righteous anger.

She wasn't vengeful, nor did she have a desire to hurt Lucas. It was simply that she was black-and-white in her thinking. They were either together or they weren't, and she couldn't bear the underlying invitation in his eyes, his voice, to be friends now that he had decreed their relationship was over. "As I recall, you were more interested in taking my clothes off than noticing what I was wearing. You had no more interest in my wardrobe than you had in any other aspect of my life."

His brows jerked together. "That's not true. You were the one who decreed we had to live separate lives."

Her hands curled into fists. "Don't say it didn't suit you."

"It did, at the time."

"Ha!" But the moment of triumph was hollow. She just wished she had realized she wasn't built for such a shallow, restricted relationship.

Pointedly, she checked her wristwatch. "I have a meeting in ten minutes. If there's nothing else, I need to go. With the product launch in two days' time, there's a lot to do."

"That's what I wanted to talk to you about. We've made some changes to the arrangements for the launch party. Nina will be heading up the team running the promotion."

Not fired, Carla thought blankly. Sidelined.

She took a deep breath and let it out slowly, but when she spoke her voice was still unacceptably husky. "Some product launch without the most high-profile component, or have you forgotten that I'm 'The Face of Ambrosi'?"

Broodingly, Lucas surveyed Carla's perfect face, exquisite in every detail from exotic eyes to delicate cheekbones and enticing mouth. Add in the outrageously sexy tousle of dark hair trailing down her back and she was spectacularly irresistible.

Ambrosi had cut costs and cashed in on Carla's appeal, but he found himself grimly annoyed every time he noticed one of the posters. "It's hard to miss when your face is plastered all over the front of the building."

And in every one of the perfumed women's magazines he had been forced to flick through since he'd stepped into Sienna Ambrosi's front office.

Triumph glowed briefly in her gaze. "You can't sideline me. I have to be there." She began ticking off all the reasons he couldn't surgically remove her from the campaign.

His frustration levels increased exponentially with every valid reason, from interviews with women's magazines to a promotional stunt she had organized.

"I have to be there—it's a no-brainer. Besides, the costuming has all been completed to my measurements."

He cut her off in midstream. "No."

Carla's eyes narrowed. "Why not?"

Not a subject he was prepared to go live on, he thought, gaze fixed on the sleek fit of her red suit.

Every time he saw one of the posters, he had to fight the irrational urge to rip it down. The idea that Carla would do a promotional show in the transparent, pearl-encrusted creation he had viewed in front of an audience filled with voyeuristic men was the only no-brainer in the equation.

Over his dead body.

He felt as proprietary as he imagined a father would feel keeping his daughter from hormonal teenage boys. Not that his feelings were remotely fatherly. She could threaten and argue all day; it wasn't going to happen.

"You haven't been well, and you could be pregnant," he said flatly. "I'll do the interviews, and I've arranged for a model to take your place for the promotion. Nina is hosting the promotional show. Elise will take care of the styling."

Styling. He gripped the taut muscles at his nape. A week ago he didn't even know what that meant.

"I'm so well I'm jumping out of my skin. I'm here to work. The launch is *my* project."

"Not anymore."

Silence hung heavy in the air. Somewhere in the office a clock ticked; out on the street someone leaned on a car horn. Carla groped for the fire-engine-red bag that matched her suit.

Lucas's stomach clenched when he saw tears glittering on her lashes. Ah, damn... He resisted the sudden off-the-wall urge to coax her close and offer comfort. He had expected opposition—a fight—but he hadn't been prepared for this level of emotion. Somewhere in the raft of detail involved with taking over Ambrosi and figuring out how to handle Carla, he had forgotten how passionately intense and protective she was about her family and the business. Although how he could forget a detail that had seen *him* sidelined in Carla's life, he didn't know. "Carla—"

"Don't." She turned on her heel.

Jaw clenched against the need to comfort her and soothe away the hurt, he reached the door first. His hand landed on the cream-and–gilt-detailed panel of the door, preventing her from opening it. "Just one more thing. My mother and Zane fly in tomorrow. I've organized a press conference to promote The Atraeus Group's takeover of Ambrosi and the product launch, then a private lunch. As a family member and PR executive your presence is required at both."

She stared blankly ahead. "Will Lilah be there?"

"Yes."

Lucas had to restrain himself from going after Carla as she strode out of his office. His jaw tightened as he noted the outrageously sexy red heels and the enticing sway of her hips as she walked. The fact that he had lost his temper was disturbing, but ten days kicking his heels while she had disappeared off the radar had set him on edge. The second he had seen her in the red suit he had lost it. He had been certain she wasn't wearing anything but a bra under the tight little jacket, and he had been right.

Closing the door, he prowled back to the window and held aside the silky curtains that draped the window, feeling like a voyeur himself as he watched Carla stroll out onto the street and climb into the sports car that was waiting for her.

He had questioned her assistant extensively about her meetings, then, dissatisfied with her answers, had looked both Chandler and Howarth up on the internet.

Elise had been correct in her summation. Both men were old enough to be her father. Unfortunately, that didn't seem to cut any ice with him. They were men, period.

At a point in time when he should have been reinforcing

the end of their relationship by keeping his distance, he had never felt more possessive or jealous.

Instead of moving to Sydney, he should have stepped back and simply kept in touch with Carla. If she was pregnant, whether she told him or not, he would soon have known. Instead he had grabbed at the excuse to be close to her.

The fact that he had lost control to the extent that he had made love to Carla after they had broken up, *without protection,* still had the power to stun him.

Worse, he found the idea that they could have made a baby together unbearably sexy and appealing.

Maybe it was a kickback to his grief and loss over Sophie, but a part of him actually hoped Carla was pregnant.

He dropped the curtain as the taxi merged into traffic. Broodingly, he reflected that when it came to Carla Ambrosi, he found himself thinking in medieval absolutes.

For two years one absolute had dominated: regardless of how risky or illogical the liaison was, he had wanted Carla Ambrosi.

Despite breaking up and replacing her with a new girlfriend—a woman he had not been able to bring himself to either touch or kiss—nothing had changed.

Seven

Carla checked the time on the digital clock in her small sports car. She had ten minutes to reach Alex Panopoulos's office and rush hour was in full swing, the traffic already jammed.

On edge and impatient, Carla used every shortcut she knew, but even so she was running late when she reached the dim underground garage.

Late for an interview that was becoming increasingly important, she grabbed her handbag and portfolio and exited the car.

Her heels tapped on concrete as she strode to the elevator, just as a sleek dark car cruised into a nearby space. The tinted driver's side window was down, giving her a shadowy glimpse of the driver. The car reminded her of the vehicle Lucas's security detail used when he was in town.

Frowning, she stepped into the elevator and keyed in the PIN she had been given. She punched the floor number, then wished she hadn't as the doors slid shut, nixing her view of the driver before he could climb out of the car. Maybe she was paranoid, or simply too focused on Lucas, but for a split second she had entertained the crazy thought that the driver could be Lucas.

She kept an eye on the floor numbers as they lit up. She caught her reflection in the polished steel doors. The scene with Lucas accusing her of dressing to entice replayed in her mind.

Hurt spiraled through her that he clearly had such a bad opinion of her and was so keen to get rid of her that he had replaced her both personally and professionally. She wondered if he intended to escort Lilah to the event, then grimly decided that of course he would.

As a publicity stunt, the move couldn't be faulted. The media would love Lilah fronting for Ambrosi and the further evidence of her close relationship with Lucas. Ambrosi couldn't ask for a better launch gimmick…except maybe an engagement announcement at the launch party.

Her chest squeezed tight on a pang of misery. Suddenly, that didn't seem as ludicrous or far-fetched as it should, given that Lucas and Lilah had only been publicly dating for a couple of weeks. Lucas was legendary for his ruthless efficiency, his unequivocal decisions. If he had decided Lilah was the one, why wait?

The elevator doors opened onto a broad carpeted corridor. Discreetly suited executives, briefcases in hand, obviously leaving for the day, stepped into the elevator as she stepped out.

The receptionist showed her into Alex's office.

Twenty minutes later, the interview over, Carla stepped out of the lift and strode to her car. She had been offered the job of PR executive for Pan Jewelry, but she had turned it down. Five minutes into the interview she had realized that

Alex hadn't wanted her expertise; he had wanted to utilize her connection with the Atraeus family. Apparently, he could double his profit base in two years if they allowed Pan to trade in the luxury Atraeus Resorts.

She had been prepared to withstand his smooth charm, possibly even reject an attempt at seduction. She had done that before, on more than one occasion. Alex had made it clear he was prepared to deal generously with her in terms of position and salary, including a free apartment, if she came to him.

Stomach churning at the sexual strings that were clearly attached to his offer, and because she had missed lunch, Carla tossed her portfolio and purse on the backseat of her car. Flipping the glove box open, she found the box of cookies she kept there for just such an emergency. Part of the reason she had ended up with an ulcer was that she had a high-acid system. She had to be careful of what she ate, and of not eating at all. Stress coupled with an empty stomach was a definite no-no. Popping a chunk of the cookie in her mouth, she drove out of the parking garage.

The car she had thought could possibly belong to Lucas's security guy was no longer in its space, but, as she took the ramp up onto the sunlit street, the distinctive dark sedan nosed in behind her.

Spine tingling with a combination of renewed anger and the flighty, unreasoning panic of knowing someone was following her—no matter how benign the reason—she sped up. The car stayed with her, confirming in her mind that it *was* one of Lucas's men snooping on her.

Still fuming at his high-handed behavior, she pulled into her apartment building. When the sedan slid past the entrance and kept on going, she reversed out and made a beeline for Lucas's inner-city apartment.

Twenty minutes later, after running the gauntlet of a concierge and one of Lucas's security detail, she pressed the buzzer on Lucas's penthouse door.

It swung open almost immediately. Lucas was still dressed in the dark pants and white shirt he had worn to the office that morning, although minus the tie and with the shirt hanging open to reveal a mouthwatering slice of taut and tanned torso. He leaned one shoulder against the door-jamb, unsubtly blocking her from barging into his apartment.

"Tell me that wasn't you following me."

"It wasn't me following you. It was Tiberio."

"In that case, do you really want to have this discussion in the hallway, where anyone can overhear?"

Cool amusement tugged at his mouth. "I rent the entire floor. The other three apartments are all occupied by my people."

"Let me rephrase that, then. Do you really want to have this discussion where your employees can overhear what I'm about to say?"

His jaw tightened, but he stepped back, leaving her just enough room to march past him. She was in the hallway, strolling across rug-strewn wooden floors into an expansive, airy sitting room before she had time to consider the unsettling fact that Lucas might not be alone. With his shirt hanging open and his sleeves unbuttoned it was highly likely he had company.

Her stomach churned at the thought. She'd had plenty of time on the drive over to consider that Lilah could be here.

She breathed a sigh of relief when she registered that the sitting room, at least, was unoccupied, although that didn't rule out the bedrooms. Until that moment she hadn't known just how much she dreaded seeing Lilah in Lucas's home, occupying the position in his life that until a few days ago she had foolishly assumed was hers.

Fingers tightening on her purse, she surveyed the sitting room with its eclectic mix of artwork and sculpture. Some she knew well; at least two she had never seen. "Nice paintings."

But then that had been one of the things that had attracted her to Lucas. He wasn't stuffy with either his thinking or his enjoyment of art.

As her gaze was drawn from one new painting to the next, absorbing the nuances of line, form and color, her stomach tensed. "A new artist?"

"You know me." His gaze was faintly mocking as he walked through an open-plan dining area to a modern kitchen and opened the fridge. "I'm always on the lookout for new talent."

It occurred to her that the artist could be Lilah, who painted in her spare time, and jealousy gripped her. Before she could stop herself she had stepped closer to the nearest of the new paintings, so she could study the signature. S. H. Crew, not L. Cole.

Her knees felt a little shaky as she moved on to the next painting, also by S. H. Crew. For some odd reason, the thought that Lilah might appeal to Lucas on a creative, spiritual level was suddenly more sharply hurtful than her physical presence would have been.

Lucas loomed over her, the warm scent of his skin, the faint undernote of sandalwood, making her pulse race. "Is it safe to give you this?"

"Not really." Jaw clenching against an instant flashback of the scene on Medinos when she had dashed water over Lucas, and the lovemaking that had followed, she took the glass of ice water. She strolled the length of the sitting room and drifted into a broad hall that served as a gallery. She sipped water and pretended to be interested in the paintings that flowed along a curving cream wall that just happened to lead to the master bedroom. "So why did you have me followed?"

He strolled past her and stood, arms folded over his chest, blocking her view of his bedroom. "I wanted to see what you were up to. Tell me," he said grimly, "what did Panopoulos offer you?"

She blinked at the mention of Panopoulos's name, but it went in one ear and out the other. She was consumed with suspicion because Lucas clearly did not want her to see into his bedroom, and the notion that Lilah was there, maybe even in his bed, was suddenly overwhelming.

Setting the water down on a narrow hall table she marched past him. Lucas's hand curled around her arm as she stepped through the door, swinging her around to face him, but not before she had ascertained that his bedroom was empty. And something else that made her heart slam hard against the wall of her chest.

What he hadn't wanted her to see. A silk robe she had left at his apartment by mistake the last time she had been here almost three months ago, and which was exactly where she had left it, draped over the back of a chair. The aquamarine silk was wildly exotic, sexy and utterly feminine. No woman would have missed its presence or significance and allowed it to remain. The robe was absolute proof that Lilah had never been in Lucas's bedroom.

Her heart beat a queer, rapid tattoo in her chest. "You haven't slept with her yet."

Lucas let her go, his gaze glittering with displeasure. "Maybe I was in the process of getting rid of your things before I invited her over."

Anger flaring, she backed up a half step. The cool solidity of the door frame stopped her dead. "I'm here now, you can hand it to me personally."

"Is that a command, or are you going to ask me nicely?"

Wary of the banked heat in Lucas's gaze, which was clearly at odds with the coolness of his tone, she controlled her temper with difficulty. "I just did ask you nicely."

"I'm willing to bet you were nicer to Alex Panopoulos when you walked into his office in that suit. Did you finally agree to sleep with him?"

"*Sleep* with him?" The words came out as an incredulous yelp. She couldn't help it, she was so utterly distracted by the fact that Lucas thought she could be even remotely interested in Alex Panopoulos, a man she barely tolerated for the sake of business. "Well, I haven't jumped into his bed, yet. Does that make you feel better about me?"

Hot anger simmered through her, doubly compounded by the humiliating fact that Panopoulos *had* wanted to sleep with her.

With a suddenness that shocked her, Lucas leaned forward and kissed her. The sensual shock of the kiss, even though she had half expected it and had goaded him into it, sent a wave of heat through Carla. Until that moment, she hadn't understood how much she had wanted to provoke him, how angry she was at his defection. She was also hurt that he still didn't know who she was after more than two years, and evidently didn't have any interest in knowing, when she was deeply, painfully in love with him.

She blinked, dazed. At some point, she realized, probably that first time they had met, something had happened. After years of dating men and knowing they weren't right, she had taken one look at Lucas and chosen him.

That was why she had broken almost every personal rule she'd had and slept with Lucas in the first place, then continued with the relationship when she knew any association with him would hurt her family. If she had been sensible and controlled she would have stepped back and waited. After all, if a relationship had legs it should stand the test of a little time. But she hadn't been able to wait. She had wanted him, needed him, right then, the same way she needed him now.

Two years. She blinked at the immensity of her self-deception. She had buried the in-love thing behind the pretense that theirs was a modern relationship between two overcommitted people with the added burden of some crazy family pressures. Anything to bury the fact that the sporadic interludes with Lucas in no way satisfied her need to be loved.

Her arms closed convulsively around his neck. She shouldn't be kissing him now, not when she wanted so much more, but in that moment she ceased to care.

"What's wrong?" Lucas pulled back, his gaze suddenly heart-stoppingly soft. "Am I hurting you?"

"No." *Yes.* Her hands tangled in the thick black silk of his hair and dragged his mouth back to hers. "Just kiss me."

Long minutes later they made it to the bed. She dragged his shirt off his shoulders and tossed it aside. Her palms slid across his sleek, heavy shoulders and muscled chest. Giddy pleasure spun through her as he removed her clothing, piece by piece, and she, in turn, removed his.

Time seemed to slow, then stop as she fitted herself against him and clasped his head, pulling his mouth to hers, needing him closer, needing him with her. Late-afternoon sun slanted through the shutters, tiger striping his shoulders as his gaze linked with hers and she suddenly knew why making love with Lucas had always been so special, so important. For those few minutes when they were truly joined it was as if he unlocked a part of himself that normally she could never quite reach, and he was wholly hers. In those few moments she could believe that he did love her.

Cool air swirled around naked skin as he sheathed himself. Relief shivered through her as they flowed together. She was utterly absorbed by the feel of him inside her, his touch and taste, the slow, thorough way he made love to her, as if he knew her intimately, as if they did belong together.

Aside from those few minutes on Medinos it had been long months since they had last made love, and she had missed him, missed this. As crazy as it seemed, despite everything that had gone wrong, everything that was still wrong, this part was right.

His head dipped, she felt the softness of his lips against her neck. Her stomach clenched, the slowly building tension suddenly unbearable as she tightened around him. She felt his raw shudder. In that moment her own climax shimmered through her with an intense pleasure that made tears burn behind her lids, and the room spun away.

Long minutes later the buzzer at the front door jerked her out of the sleepy doze she had fallen into. With smooth, fluid movements, Lucas rolled out of bed, snagged his clothes off the floor and walked through to the adjoining bathroom. Seconds later, he reappeared, fastening dark trousers around narrow hips as he strolled to the door.

Carla didn't wait to see who it was. Snatching up her clothes, including her bra, which had ended up hooked over a bedside lamp, she hurried into the bathroom to freshen up and change. Her clothes were crumpled and her hair was a tumbled mass, but she couldn't worry about that. Her priority was to leave as quickly as possible.

Slipping into her shoes, she searched and found her bag on the floor just outside the bedroom door. She must have dropped it when Lucas had kissed her there. Her cheeks burned with embarrassment as she marched through the sitting room where Lucas was talking in low, rapid Medinian to two of his security personnel.

Lucas said her name. She ignored him and the curious looks of the men, in favor of sliding through the open door and making a dash for the elevator.

Relief eased some of her tension when she saw that the doors were open. Jogging inside, she jabbed the ground floor button as Lucas appeared in the corridor.

"Wait," he said curtly.

The doors closed an instant before he reached the elevator. Heart pounding, Carla examined her reflection in the mirrored rear wall and spent the few seconds repairing her smudged mascara. She winced at her swollen lips and the pink mark on her neck where Lucas's stubble must have grazed her. She looked as if she had just rolled out of bed.

The elevator stopped with a faint jolt. Shoving her mascara back in her bag, Carla strolled quickly through the foyer, ignoring the concierge, who stared at her with a fascinated expression.

She almost stopped dead when she saw Lilah sitting in a chair, flipping through a magazine, obviously waiting. Pretending she hadn't noticed her, Carla quickened her step. Now the two security staff talking with Lucas in hushed, rapid Medinian made sense. Lilah had wanted to go up to Lucas's apartment, but they had known Carla was there.

Mortified, she dimly registered Lilah's white face, the shock in her eyes, as she pushed the foyer doors wide. The sound of traffic hit her like a blow. The sun, now low on the horizon, shone directly in her eyes, dazzling her, a good excuse for the tears stinging her eyes. Her throat tightened as she started down the front steps.

As she stepped onto the sidewalk a hand curved around her arm, stopping her in her tracks.

Her heart did a queer leap in her chest as she spun. "Lucas."

Eight

Carla wrenched free. Lucas was still minus his shirt, his hair sexily tangled. If she looked rumpled, he definitely looked like he had just rolled out of the love nest. "How did you get down so fast?"

"There's a second, private lift."

Her fingers tightened on the strap of her bag. "More to the point, why did you bother?"

His gaze narrowed. "I won't glorify that with an answer. What did you think you were doing running out like that?"

Now that the initial shock of Lucas chasing after her was over, she was desperate to be gone. She needed to be alone so she could stamp out the crazy notion that kept sliding into her mind that there was still a chance for them. She had to get it through her skull that there was no hope. She was the one who got lost in useless emotion, while Lucas remained coolly elusive.

Her gaze flashed. "We were finished, weren't we?" *In*

more ways than one. "Or was there something else you wanted?"

Heat burned along his cheekbones. "You know I never viewed you that way."

"How, then?"

He said something low and taut in Medinian that she was pretty sure was a swear word or phrase of some kind. Not for the first time it occurred to her that for her own peace of mind she really should learn some of that language.

His palm curved around the base of her neck, his fingers tangling in her hair. A split second later his mouth closed over hers.

A series of flashes, the slick, motorized clicking of a high-speed camera jerked them apart. A reporter with an expensive-looking camera had just emerged from a parked car.

A shudder of horror swept Carla. When the press recognized her they would put one and one together and make seven. Before she arrived back at her apartment they would have her entangled in a second-time-around affair with Lucas. By morning they would have her cast off and pregnant or, more probably, since Lucas was involved with Lilah, caught up in some trashy love triangle.

Most of it, unfortunately, was embarrassingly true.

A strangled sound jerked her head around. Bare meters away, directly behind Lucas, Lilah was caught in an awkward freeze-frame.

Carla's stomach lurched as if she'd just stepped into a high-speed elevator on its way down. That was a definite "go" on the love triangle.

Lilah spun on her heel and walked quickly away.

With a final, manic series of clicks the reporter slid back into the car from which he had emerged. With a high-pitched whine reminiscent of a kitchen appliance the tiny hatchback sped away.

Lucas swore softly, this time in English, and released his grip on her nape. His gaze was weary. "Did you know he was out here?"

Her temper soared at what she could only view as an accusation. She gestured at her crumpled clothing and hair, the smeared makeup. "Do I look like I'm ready to be photographed by some sleazy tabloid reporter?"

Lucas's brows jerked together. "You did it once before."

A tide of heat swept her at his reference to her admittedly outrageous behavior in making their first breakup public and the resulting scandal that had followed. "You deserved that for the way you treated me."

"I apologized."

He had apologized. And she had forgiven him, then continued to sleep with him. There was a pattern there, somewhere.

His head jerked around as he spotted Lilah climbing into a small sedan. Slipping a cell phone out of his pants pocket, he punched in a number.

Carla blinked at his sudden change of focus. Feeling oddly deflated and emptied of emotion, she rummaged in her purse to find her car keys. "Before you ask the question, the reporter didn't follow me. Why would he? I'm not your girlfriend."

Lucas frowned and gave up on the call, which clearly wasn't being picked up.

He was no doubt calling Lilah, trying to soothe her hurt and explain away his mistake. Despite the fact that Carla knew she was the one in the wrong for sleeping with Lucas, she found she couldn't bear the thought of Lucas trivializing what they had just shared.

He had the nerve to try the phone number again.

A red mist swam before her eyes. Before she even registered what she was about to do, her hand shot out, closed around the phone and she flung it as hard as she could onto the road. It bounced and flew into several pieces. A split second later a truck ran over the main body of the phone, smashing it flat.

There was a moment of silence.

Lucas's expression was curiously devoid of emotion. "That was an expensive phone."

"So sue me, but I find it insulting and objectionable that the man I've just slept with should phone another woman in my presence. You could have at least waited until I had left."

His gaze narrowed. "My apologies for accusing you of calling the press in. I forgot about Lilah."

"Something you seem to be doing a lot lately. I don't know what you're doing out here with me when you should be concentrating on getting back with her."

A swirling breeze started up, making her feel chilled. She rubbed at the gooseflesh on her arms, suddenly in urgent need of a hot bath and an early night. Technically, she was still recovering from the viral relapse and under doctor's orders to take it easy, not that she would tell Lucas that. She was supposed to take an afternoon nap if she could fit it in. Ha!

She started toward her car. Lucas stepped in front of her, blocking her path.

She stared at his sleek, bare shoulders and muscled chest, the dark line of hair that arrowed down to the waistband of his pants. She was tired, and her body still ached and throbbed in places from what they had done in his penthouse apartment. What they had done was *wrong*, but that didn't stop the automatic hum of desire.

"I have no plans on 'getting back' with Lilah. Do you intend to sleep with Panopoulos?"

She went still inside at the first part of that sentence, although she felt no sense of surprise that Lucas was breaking up with Lilah. If he could gravitate back to her so easily then clearly there wasn't much holding them together. Then a second thunderbolt hit her.

Lucas was jealous.

Make that *very* jealous. She didn't know why she hadn't seen it before, but the knowledge demystified his overbearing reaction to her job interview with Alex Panopoulos. It also cast a new light on the dictatorial way he had decided that she would no longer be "The Face" or act in the promotional play she had planned to stage as part of Ambrosi's product launch. She had thought he was downgrading her both personally and professionally because he didn't want her, but the opposite was true.

A glow of purely feminine pleasure soothed over the hurt he had inflicted by demoting her. The launch was *her* baby. She had meticulously planned every detail, always shooting for perfection, and she needed to be there to make sure everything went smoothly. She still didn't like what he had done, but she understood his reasoning now and, because it involved his emotions for her, she would allow him to get away with being so high-handed.

Her chin came up at the question about Alex Panopoulos, although it no longer had any sting. "You're not my boyfriend," she said flatly. "You have no right to ask that question."

Maybe not. But that situation was about to change.

Lucas's jaw locked as he controlled the surge of cold fury at the thought of Carla and Panopoulos together. When he had asked her before she had said she hadn't slept with him, and he believed her, but he knew Alex Panopoulos. He was wealthy and spoiled and used to having what he wanted. If he wanted Carla, he wouldn't give up.

His hands curled into fists at the almost overwhelming urge to simply pick Carla up and carry her back up to his apartment and his bed. Instead, he forced himself to stillness as Carla climbed behind the wheel of her sports car and shot away from the curb.

He was finished with caveman tactics. Finesse was now required.

He examined his options as he took the stairs into his apartment building and strode through the foyer. They were not black-and-white, exactly, but close.

He stepped into the elevator, which Tiberio was holding for him. It was a fact that ever since he had first seen Carla he hadn't been able to keep his hands off her. His attempt to create distance and sever their relationship had backfired. Instead of killing his desire, distance had only served to increase it to the point that the very thing he had been trying to avoid happened: he lost control.

He could deny the story the tabloids would print and which would no doubt hit the stands by morning, or he could allow the story to stand. If he took the second option, Carla's name would be dragged through the mud. He would not allow that to happen.

Until that afternoon, he had been certain about the one thing he didn't want: a forced marriage to Carla Ambrosi.

But that had been before she had waved Alex Panopoulos in his face.

The elevator door slid open. Jaw tight, Lucas strode to his apartment and waited for Tiberio to swipe the key card.

He walked through to his bedroom, every muscle locking tight as he studied the rumpled bed. He picked up the sexy, exotic silk wrap, his fingers closing on the silk. Her delicate feminine scent still clung to the silk, the same scent that currently permeated the very air of his room and would now be in his bed.

If she had wanted to force his hand, he reflected, she could have done it at the beginning, when the media had published the story about the first night they had spent together. Instead, she had walked away from him. He was the one who'd had to do the running.

He had gotten her back, but only after weeks of effort. His fingers tightened on the silk. It was an uncomfortable fact that he wanted Carla more now than he had in the beginning. With each encounter, instead of weakening, his need had intensified.

Now Panopoulos had entered the picture.

Alex was a clever man who had leveraged a modest fortune into an impressive retail empire. Lucas was aware that he wouldn't miss the opportunity to enhance his bid to place his stores in Atraeus resorts by marrying close to his family.

Lucas reached for his cell phone, and remembered that Carla had destroyed it. He shook his head at the irrational urge to grin. The destruction of personal property, especially his, shouldn't be viewed as sexy.

He found the landline then, irritated because his directory had been on his dead cell and he had to ring his PA on Medinos to find the unlisted number. Frustrating minutes later, he made the call. Panopoulos picked up almost immediately.

Lucas's message was succinct and direct.

If Panopoulos offered Carla any kind of position within his company, or laid so much as a finger on her, he would lose any chance at a business alliance with The Atraeus Group. Lucas would also see to it personally that a lucrative business deal Panopoulos was currently negotiating with a European firm The Atraeus Group had a stake in, deVries, would be withdrawn.

Panopoulos's voice was clipped. "Are you warning me off because Constantine is now married to Carla's sister?"

"No." Lucas made no effort to temper the cold flatness of his reply. "Because Carla Ambrosi is mine."

The instant he said the words satisfaction curled through him. Decision made.

Carla was his. Exclusively his.

He was over making excuses to be with her. He wanted her. And he would do what he had to to make sure that not Panopoulos or any other man went near her again.

Terminating the call, Lucas propped the phone back on its rest.

Panopoulos was smart; he would back off. Now all Lucas had to do was talk to Lilah, then deal with the press and Carla.

Carla wouldn't like his ultimatum, but she would accept it. The damage had been done in the instant the reporter had snapped them on the street.

The following morning, after a mostly sleepless night, Carla dressed for the scheduled press conference and luncheon with care. Bearing in mind the elegance of the restaurant Lucas had booked, she chose a pale blue dress that looked spectacular against her skin and hair. It was also subtly sexy in the way it skimmed her curves and revealed a hint of cleavage. High, strappy blue heels made her legs look great, and a classy little jacket in powder-blue finished off the outfit.

Normally she would dress in a more low-key way for a press conference, but any kind of meeting with Lucas today called for a special effort. The heels were a tad high, but that wasn't a problem; she had learned to balance on four-inch stilettos from an early age. She figured that by now that particular ability was imprinted in her DNA.

She decided to leave her hair loose, but took extra care with her makeup in an effort to hide the faint shadows under her eyes.

Minutes later, after sipping her way through a cup of coffee, she stepped out of her apartment. As she locked the door, she noticed a familiar sleek sedan parked across the entrance to her driveway, blocking her in. Her tiredness evaporated on a surge of displeasure.

As she marched toward the car she could make out the shadowy outline of a man behind darkly tinted windows. It would be one of Lucas's security team, probably the guy who had tailed her to her interview with Alex Panopoulos.

Temper escalating, she bent down and tapped on the passenger-side window. Tinted glass slid down with an expensive hum. Glittering dark eyes locked with hers and a short, sharp jab of adrenaline shot through her. Lucas.

Dressed in a gray suit with a metallic sheen and a black T-shirt, his hair still damp from his shower, Lucas looked broodingly attractive. His hair was rumpled as if he'd run his fingers through it. He looked edgy and irritable, the shadow on his jaw signaling that he hadn't had time to shave.

The irritating awareness that still dogged her despite her repeated efforts to reprogram her mind kicked in, making her belly clench and her jaw set even tighter. "What are you doing here?"

"Keeping the press off." Lucas jerked his head in the direction of a blue hatchback parked on the opposite side of the street.

With an unpleasant start, Carla recognized the reporter who had snapped them outside Lucas's apartment the previous evening. "He wouldn't be here if he wasn't following you."

"He arrived before I did."

Her stomach sank. That meant the press would be going

all out with whatever story they could leverage out of that kiss. "Even more reason for you not to be here."

He leaned over and opened the passenger door. "Get in."

Carla gauged the time it would take to dash to her small garage, open the door and back her convertible out. With the reporter just a few fast steps away it would be no contest.

The flash and whir of the camera sent a second shot of adrenaline zinging through her veins as she slid into the passenger seat and slammed the door. The thunk of the locks engaging coincided with the throaty roar of the engine as the vehicle shot away from the curb. Seconds later, they were on the motorway heading into town and forced to an agonizing crawl by rush-hour traffic.

Carla relaxed her death grip on her purse, strapped on her seat belt and checked the rearview mirror. Anything but acknowledge the fact that she was once more within touching distance of Lucas Atraeus.

And riding in his car.

Although this wasn't his personal car. His taste usually ran to something a little more muscular and a lot faster, like the Maserati, but the intimacy still set her on edge and recalled one too many memories she would rather forget.

The first time they had made love had been in a car.

Two years ago he had given her a lift home from a dinner at a restaurant, a family meet-and-greet following Constantine and Sienna's first engagement.

Accepting a lift with Lucas, when she had expected to be delivered home the same way she had arrived, via hired limousine service, had seemed safe despite his bad-boy reputation with the tabloids. Plus there was the fact that recently he had been photographed on two separate occasions, each time with a different gorgeous girl.

Despite telling herself that he was clearly not on the hunt, when she slid into his car, she had felt a deliciously edgy kind of thrill. Lucas was gorgeous in a dangerous, masculine way, so she was more than a little flattered to be singled out for his attention.

It had taken a good half hour to reach her apartment during which time Lucas had played cruising music and asked her about her family and whether or not she was dating.

When they'd reached her place it was pitch-dark. Instead of parking out on the street, Lucas had driven right up to her garage door and parked beneath the shelter of a large shade tree. An oak overhung the driveway and blocked the neighbor's view on one side. Her security lights had flicked on as Lucas turned off the engine, although they remained encapsulated in darkness since the garage blocked the light from reaching the car.

With the music gone, the silence took on a heavy intensity, and her stomach had tightened on a kick of nerves because she knew in that moment that despite her frantic reasoning to the contrary, he *did* want to kiss her. If Lucas was just dropping her home, he wouldn't have driven right into her driveway, and so far up it that the car was partially concealed.

He had barely touched her all night, although she had been aware that he had been watching her and, admittedly, she had played to her audience.

But all of the time she had flirted and played she had been on edge in a feminine way, her nerves tingling. She was used to being pursued, that went with the fashion industry and the PR job. But Lucas was in a whole different league and she hadn't made up her mind that she wanted him to catch her.

She had turned her head, bracing herself for the jolt of eye contact, and his mouth caught hers, his tongue siding right in. A burning shaft of heat shot straight to her loins and she went limp.

Long seconds later, he had released her mouth. She gulped in air and then his mouth closed on hers again and she was sinking, drowning. Her arms closed convulsively around his neck, her fingers tangling in his hair, which was thick and silky and just long enough to play with. Not a good idea, since playing with Lucas Atraeus was the dating equivalent of stroking a big hunting cat, but the second he had touched her, her normal rules had evaporated.

She'd felt the zipper of her silk sheath being eased down her spine, the hot shock of his fingers against the bare skin of her back.

He'd muttered something in Medinian, too thick and rapid for her to catch, and lifted his head, jaw taut. "Do you want this?"

She realized he was holding on to control by a thread. The realization of his vulnerability was subtly shocking.

From the first her connection with Lucas had been powerful. Cliché or not, she had literally glanced across the restaurant and been instantly riveted.

Head and shoulders above most of the occupants of the room, all three Atraeus brothers had been compelling, but it had been Lucas's faintly battered profile that had drawn her.

She had let out a shuddering breath, abruptly aware of what he was asking. Not just a kiss. Somehow they had already stepped way beyond a kiss.

He'd bent his head as if he couldn't bear not to touch her. His lips feathered her throat, sending hot rills of sensation chasing across her skin, and abruptly something slotted into place in her mind.

She had been twenty-four, and a virgin, not because she had been consciously celibate but for the simple reason that she had never met anyone with whom she wanted to be that intimate. No matter how much she liked a date, if they couldn't knock her sideways emotionally, she refused to allow anything more than a good-night kiss.

Making love with Lucas Atraeus hadn't made sense for

a whole list of logical reasons. She barely knew him, and so there was no way she could be in love, but instead of recoiling, she'd found herself irresistibly compelled to throw away her rule book. On an instinctive level, with every touch, every kiss, Lucas Atraeus felt utterly right. "Yes."

A car horn blasted, shattering the recall, jerking Carla's gaze back to the road.

"What's wrong?"

Lucas's deep, raspy voice sent a nervy shock wave through her. His gaze caught hers, dispatching another electrical jolt. "Nothing."

His phone vibrated. He answered the call, his voice low. A couple of times his gaze intercepted hers and that weird electrical hum of awareness zapped her again, so she switched back to watching the wing mirror. Once she thought she spotted the blue hatchback and she stiffened, but she couldn't be certain.

"He's not behind us. I've been checking."

Which raised a question. "You said he got to my place before you did, so how did you know he was there?"

Constantine inched forward in traffic, braked, then reached behind to the backseat and handed her a newspaper, which had been folded open.

The headline, Lightning Strikes Twice for Atraeus Hatchet Man, sent her into mild shock, although she had been expecting something like it.

They hadn't made the front page, but close. A color photo, which had been taken just as Lucas had kissed her, was slotted directly below the story title.

Her outrage built as she skimmed the piece. According to the reporter, the romantic fires had been reignited during a secret tryst while she'd been on Medinos. An "insider" had supplied the tidbit that the wedding had literally thrown them together and they were now a hot romantic item. Again.

Although the speculation that Lucas would pop the question was strictly lighthearted. According to the "source," if Carla Ambrosi hadn't had what it took to keep Atraeus interested the first time around, the "reheat" would be about as exciting as day-old pasta.

Carla dropped the newspaper as if it had scorched her fingers. The instant she had seen her name coupled with Lucas's she should have known better than to read on.

Two years ago when Lucas had finished with her after that one night, she had been angry enough to go to the press. They'd had a field day with speculation and innuendo. Her skin was a lot thicker now, but the careless digging into her personal life, and the outright lies, still stung.

Reheat.

Her jaw tightened. If she ever found out who the cowardly "insider" was, the next installment of that particular story could be printed in the crime pages.

Folding the newspaper, she tossed it on the backseat. "You should have called me. You didn't have to show up on my doorstep."

Making it look like there really was substance to the story.

"If I'd called, you would have hung up on me."

She couldn't argue with that, because it was absolutely true.

Lucas signaled and made a turn into the underground parking garage beneath the Ambrosi building.

Carla was halfway out of the car, dragging her bag, which had snagged on a tiny lever at the base of the seat, when movement jerked her head up. A man with a camera loomed out of the shadows, walking swiftly toward them. Not the guy in the blue hatchback, someone else. The pale gleam of a van with its garish news logo registered in the background.

Lucas, who had walked around to open her door, said

something curt beneath his breath as she yanked at the strap. The bag came free and she surged upright.

"Smile, Mr. Atraeus, Ms. Ambrosi. Gotcha!"

The camera flashed as she lurched into Lucas.

The touching was minimal—her shoulder bumped his, he reached out to steady her—but the damage was done. In addition to the kiss outside Lucas's apartment the tabloids now had photos of Lucas picking her up from her apartment then delivering her to work.

The day-old pasta had just gotten hotter.

Nine

When Carla stepped out of her office to attend the press conference later on that morning, one of Lucas's bodyguards, Tiberio, was waiting for her in the corridor.

Lucas wasn't in the office. He had left after dropping her off that morning, so there was no one to interpret. After a short, labored struggle with Tiberio's fractured English, Carla finally agreed that, yes, they would both follow Lucas's orders and Tiberio could drive her to the press conference and see her safely inside.

On the way down to the parking garage, she decided that she was secretly glad Lucas had delegated Tiberio to mind her. She had been dreading dealing with the paparazzi when she arrived at the five-star hotel where the press conference was being held.

To her surprise, Tiberio opened the door on a glossy black limousine, not the dark sedan Lucas's security usually drove. When she slid into the leather interior, she was startled to discover that Lucas was already ensconced there, a briefcase open on the floor, a sheaf of papers in his hand.

The door closed, sealing her in. Lucas said something rapid to Tiberio as he slid behind the wheel. There was a discreet thunk, followed by the low hum of the engine.

She depressed the door handle, when it wouldn't budge, her gaze clashed with Lucas's. "You locked it."

His expression was suspiciously bland. "Standard security precaution."

Daylight replaced the gloom of the parking garage as they glided up onto the street. Her uneasiness at finding Lucas in the car coalesced into suspicion; she was beginning to feel manipulated. "Tiberio said you had ordered him to mind me, that he was supposed to drop me at the press conference. He didn't say we would be traveling together."

Lucas, still dressed in the silver-gray suit and black T-shirt he had been wearing that morning, but now freshly shaved, retrieved a cell phone from his briefcase. "Is there a problem with going together?"

She frowned. "After what happened, wouldn't it be the smart thing to arrive separately?"

Lucas's attention was centered on what was, apparently, a swanky new phone. "No."

Her frustration spiked as he punched in a number and lifted the phone to his ear then subsided just as quickly as she listened to his deep voice, the liquid cadences of his rapid Medinian. Reluctantly fascinated, she hung on every word. He could be reciting a grocery list and she could still listen all day.

Minutes later, the limousine pulled into a space outside the hotel entrance. When she saw the media crush, she experienced a rare moment of panic. Publicity was her thing; she had a natural bent for it. But not today. "Isn't there a back entrance we can use?"

Lucas, seemingly unconcerned, snapped his phone closed and slipped it into his pocket.

She flashed him an irritated look. "The last thing we need right now is to be seen arriving together, looking like we *are* a couple."

"Don't worry, the media will be taken care of. It's all arranged."

Something about his manner brought her head up, sharpened all her senses. "What do you mean, 'arranged'? If the media doesn't see me for a few days, the story will die a death."

"No, it won't," Lucas said flatly. "Not this time."

The door to the limousine popped open. Lucas exited first. Reluctantly Carla followed, stepping into the dusty, steamy heat of midtown Sydney.

The media surged forward. To Carla's relief they were instantly held at bay by a wall of burly men in dark suits.

Lucas's hand landed in the small of her back, the heat of his palm burning through her dress, then they were moving. Carla kept her spine stiff, informing Lucas that she wasn't happy with either the situation or his touch, which seemed entirely too intimate.

The glass doors of the hotel threw a reflection back at her. Lucas stood tall and muscled by her side, his gaze with that grim, icy quality that always sent shivers down her spine. With the other men flanking them in a protective curve, she couldn't help thinking they looked like a trailer for a gangster flick.

The doors slid open, and the air-conditioned coolness of the hotel foyer flowed around her as they walked briskly to a bank of elevators. A security guard was holding an empty elevator car. Relief eased some of her tension as they stepped inside.

Before the doors could slide closed a well-dressed female reporter, microphone in hand, cameraman in tow, side-stepped security and grabbed the door, preventing it from closing.

"Mr. Atraeus, Ms. Ambrosi, can you confirm the rumor that Sienna Atraeus is pregnant?"

There was a moment of confusion as security reacted, forcing the woman and her cameraman to step back.

Lucas issued a sharp order. The doors snapped closed and she found herself alone with Lucas as the elevator lurched into motion.

Carla's stomach clenched at the sudden acceleration.

Sienna pregnant.

"Constantine phoned me earlier to let me know that Sienna was pregnant and that it was possible the story had been leaked."

A hurt she had stubbornly avoided dealing with hit her like a kick in the chest.

She didn't begrudge Sienna one moment of her happiness, but it was a fact that she possessed all the things that Carla realized *she* wanted. Not necessarily right now, but sometime in the future, in their natural order, and with Lucas.

But Lucas was showing no real signs of commitment.

Blankly, she watched floor numbers flash by. If she were pregnant she had to assume there would be no marriage, no happy ending, no husband to love and cherish her and the child.

She became aware the elevator had stopped. She sucked in a deep breath, but the oxygen didn't seem to be getting through. Her head felt heavy and pressurized, her knees wobbly. Not illness, just good old-fashioned panic.

Lucas took her arm, holding her steady. The top of her head bumped his chin, the scrape of his stubbled jaw on the sensitive skin of her forehead sending a reflexive shiver through her. She inhaled, gasping air like a swimmer surfacing, and his warm male scent, laced with the subtle edge of cologne, filled her nostrils.

Lucas said something curt in Medinian. "Damn, you *are* pregnant."

A split second later the elevator doors slid open.

Fingers automatically tightening around the strap of her handbag, which was in danger of sliding off her shoulder, she stepped out into a broad, carpeted corridor. Lucas's security, who must have taken another elevator, were waiting.

Lucas's hand closed around her arm. "Slow down. I've got you."

"That's part of the problem."

"Then deal with it. I'm not going away."

She shot him an icy glare. "I thought leaving was the whole point?"

He traded a cool glance but didn't reply because they had reached the designated suite. A murmur rippled through the room as they were recognized, but this time, courtesy of the heavy presence of security, there was no undisciplined rush.

Tomas, Constantine's PA, and Lucas's mother, Maria Therese, were already seated. Carla took a seat next to Lucas. Seconds later, Zane escorted Lilah into the room.

Her stomach contracted as the questions began. The presence of a mediator limited the topics to the Atraeus takeover of Ambrosi, Ambrosi's new collection and the re-creation of the historic Ambrosi pearl facility on the Medinian island of Ambrus. However, when Lucas rose to his feet, indicating that the press conference was over, a barrage of personal questions ensued.

Lucas's fingers laced with hers, the contact intimate and unsettling as he pulled her to her feet. When she discreetly tried to pull free, wary of creating even more unpleasant speculation, he sent her a warning glance, his hold firming.

As they stepped off the podium the media, no longer quietly seated, swirled around them. The clear, husky voice of a well-known television reporter cut through the shouted questions. A microphone was thrust at Lucas's face.

The reporter flashed him a cool smile. "Can you confirm or deny the reports that you've resumed your affair with Carla?"

Lucas pulled her in close against his side as they continued to move at a steady pace. His gaze intersected with hers, filled with cool warning. "No official statement has been issued yet, however I can confirm that Carla Ambrosi and I have been secretly engaged for the past two years."

The room erupted. Lucas bit out a grim order. The security team, already working to push the press back, closed in, forcing a bubble of privacy and shoving Carla up hard against Lucas. His arm tightened and she found herself lifted off her feet as he literally propelled her from the room.

Shock and a wave of edgy heat zapped through her as she clung to his narrow waist and scrambled to keep her balance. Seconds later they were sealed into the claustrophobic confines of what looked like a service elevator, still surrounded by burly security.

Carla twisted, trying to peel loose from his hold. Lucas easily resisted the attempt, tightening his arms around her. In the process she ended up plastered against his chest. The top button of her dress came unfastened and his hand, which was spread across her rib cage, shifted up so that his thumb and index finger sank into the swell of one breast.

As if a switch had been thrown, she was swamped by memories, some hot and sensuous enough that her breasts tightened and her belly contracted, some hurtful enough that her temper roared to life.

Lucas's gaze burned over the lush display of cleavage where the bodice of her dress gaped. "Keep still," he growled.

But she noticed he didn't move his hand.

She was *not* enjoying it. After the humiliation of the previous evening the last thing she needed was to be clamped against all that hot, hard muscle, making her feel small and wimpy and tragically easy. Unfortunately, her body wasn't in sync with her mind. She couldn't control the heat flushing her skin or the automatic tightening of her nipples, and Lucas knew it.

The doors slid open. Before she could protest, they were moving again, this time through the lower bowels of the hotel. A door off a loading bay was shoved wide and they spilled out onto a walled parking area where several vehicles, including a limousine, were parked.

Her fury increased. Here was the back entrance she had needed an hour ago.

Hot, clammy air flowed around her as she clambered into the limousine, clutching her purse. Lucas slid in beside her, his muscled thigh brushing hers. She flinched as if scalded and scooted over another few inches.

His gaze flashed to hers as they accelerated away from the curb. "All right?"

His calm control pushed her over the edge. She reached for her seat belt and jammed the fastenings together. "Secretly *engaged?*"

A week ago an engagement was what she had longed for, what she would have *loved.* "Correct me if I'm wrong, maybe I blacked out at some stage, but I don't ever remember a proposal of marriage."

She caught Tiberio's surprised glance in the rearview mirror.

Lucas's expression was grim. A faint hum filled the air as a privacy screen slid smoothly into place, locking them into a bubble of silence.

She stared at Lucas, incensed. Thanks to the mad dash

through the hotel, her hair had unwound and was now cascading untidily down her back, and she was perspiring. In contrast, Lucas looked cool and completely in control, his suit *GQ* perfect. "An engagement is the logical solution."

"It's damage control, and it's completely unnecessary." She remembered her gaping bodice and hurriedly refastened the button. "I may not be pregnant."

Her voice sounded husky and tight, even to herself, and she wondered, a little wildly, if he could tell how much she suddenly wanted to be pregnant.

"Whether you're pregnant or not is a consideration, but it isn't an issue, yet."

Something seized in her chest, her heart. For a crazy moment she considered that he was about to admit that he was in love with her, that he didn't care if she was pregnant or not, he couldn't live without her. Then reality dissolved that fantasy. "But what the newspapers are printing is. Do you know how humiliating it is to be offered a forced marriage?"

Irritation tinged with outrage registered in his expression. "No one's *forcing* you to do anything. Marriage as an option can't be such a shock. Not after what happened on Medinos. And last night."

"Well, I guess that puts things in perspective. It's a *practical* option."

Her mood was definitely spiraling down. Practicality spelled death for all romance. Cancel the white wedding with champagne and rose petals. Bring on the registry office and matching gray suits.

"I wouldn't propose marriage if I didn't *want* to marry you."

Her gaze narrowed. "Is that the proposal?"

His expression was back to remote. "It isn't what I had planned, but, yes."

"Uh-huh." She drew a deep breath and counted to ten.

"The biggest mistake I made was in agreeing to sleep with you."

Suddenly he was close, one arm draped behind her, his warm male scent laced with the enticing cologne stopping the breath in her throat. "On which occasion?"

She stared rigidly ahead, trying to ignore the heated gleam in his eyes, the subtle cajoling that shouldn't succeed in getting her on side, but which was slowly undermining her will to resist.

That was the other thing about Lucas, besides the power and influence he wielded in the business world. When he wanted he could be stunningly seducingly attentive. But this time she refused to be swayed by his killer charm. "All of them."

He wound a strand of her hair around one finger and lightly tugged. She felt his breath fanning her nape. "That's a lot of mistakes."

And she had enjoyed every one of them.

She resisted the urge to turn her head, putting her mouth bare inches from his and letting the conversation take them to the destination he was so blatantly angling for—a bone-melting kiss. "I should never have slept with you, period."

He dropped the strand of hair and sat back, slightly, signaling that he had changed tack. "Meaning that if you had played your cards right," he said softly, "you could have had marriage in the beginning?"

Ten

Like quicksilver the irresistible pull of attraction was gone, replaced by wrenching hurt. "Just because I didn't talk about marriage, that didn't mean I thought it would never be on the agenda for us. And what is so wrong with that?"

Silence vibrated through the limousine. She saw Tiberio glance nervously in the rearview mirror. She turned her head to watch city traffic zip by and registered that her stomach felt distinctly hollow.

Glancing at her watch, she noted the time. She'd only had coffee for breakfast and it was after one. She would be eating lunch soon, which would fix the acid in her stomach, but she couldn't wait that long. Fumbling in her purse, she took out the small plastic bag that contained a few antacid tablets and a couple of individually packaged biscuits. After unwrapping a slightly battered biscuit, she took a bite.

"Marriage is on the agenda now," Lucas reminded her. "I need an answer."

She hastily finished the biscuit and stuffed the plastic bag back in her purse.

Lucas watched her movements with an annoyed fascination. "Do you usually eat when marriage is being proposed?"

"I was hungry. I needed to eat."

"I'll have to remember that should I ever have occasion to propose again."

She closed the flap on her purse. Maybe it was childish not to tell him that she had ended up with an ulcer, but it was no big deal and she was still hurt that he hadn't ever bothered to check up on her after he had deposited her on the plane home from Thailand. The memory of his treatment of her, which had been uncharacteristically callous, stiffened her spine. "I don't know why you want marriage now when clearly you broke up with me because you didn't view me as 'wife' material."

His gaze was unwavering, making her feel suddenly uncomfortable about giving him such a hard time.

"As it happens, you've always fulfilled the most important requirement."

She was suddenly, intensely conscious of the warmth of his arm behind her. "Which is?"

Her breath seized in her throat as Lucas cupped her chin with his free hand. She had a split second to either pull back or turn her head so his mouth would miss hers. Instead, hope turned crazy cartwheels in her stomach, and she allowed the kiss.

Long, breathless minutes later he lifted his head. "You wanted to know why marriage is acceptable to me. This is why."

His thumb traced the line of her cheekbone, sending tingling heat shivering across the delicate skin and igniting a familiar, heated tension. His mouth brushed hers again, the kiss lingering. The stirring tension wound tighter. Reflexively, she leaned closer, angling her jaw to deepen the kiss. Her hand slid around to grip his nape and pull him closer still.

When he finally lifted his head, his gaze was bleak. "Two months without you was two months too long. What happened on Medinos and in my apartment is a case in point. I want you back."

Carla released her hold on his nape and drew back. Her mouth, her whole body, was tingling.

It wasn't what she wanted to hear, but the hope fizzing inside refused to die a complete death.

Lucas had tried to end their relationship; it hadn't happened. She hadn't chased him. If he had truly wanted an end, she was in no doubt that he would have icily and clinically cut her out of his life.

He hadn't been able to because he couldn't resist her.

He might label what held them together as sex; she preferred to call it chemistry. There was a reason they were attracted to each other that went way beyond the physical into the area of personality and emotional needs. Despite their difficulties and clashes, at a deep, bedrock level she knew they were perfect for each other.

That they had continued their relationship for two years was further proof that whatever he either claimed or denied, for Lucas she was different in some way. She knew, because she had made it her business to check. Lucas was only ever recorded by the tabloids as having one serious relationship before her, a model called Sophie, and that had been something like five years ago. The fact that he wanted the marriage now, when a pregnancy was by no means certain, underlined just how powerfully he did want her.

It wasn't love, but everything in her shouted that it had to be possible for the potent chemistry that had bound Lucas to her for the past two years to turn to love.

She was clutching at straws. Her heart was pounding and her stomach kept lurching. There was a possibility that Lucas might never truly love her, never fully commit himself to the relationship. There was a chance she was making the biggest mistake of her life.

But, risky or not, if she was honest, her mind had been made up the second she'd heard his announcement to the press.

She loved Lucas.

If there was a chance that he could love her, then she was taking it.

Lucas activated the privacy screen. When it opened, he leaned forward and spoke in rapid Medinian to Tiberio. He caught the skeptical flash of his chief bodyguard's gaze in the rearview mirror as he confirmed that they would be making the scheduled stop at the jewelers.

However, the wry amusement that would normally have kicked up the corners of his mouth in answer to Tiberio's pessimism was absent. When it came to Carla, he was beginning to share Tiberio's doubts. She hadn't said yes, and he was by no means certain that she would.

Carla, who was once again rummaging in her handbag, stiffened as the limousine pulled into the cramped loading bay of a downtown building. "This isn't the restaurant."

Lucas climbed out as Tiberio opened the door then leaned in and took Carla's hand. "We have one stop to make before lunch."

As Carla climbed out he noted the moment she spotted the elegant sign that indicated this was the rear entrance to the premises of Moore's, a famous jeweler. A business that just happened to be owned by The Atraeus Group.

Her expression was accusing. "You had this all planned."

"Last night you knew as well as I that the story would go to press."

Her light blue gaze flashed. Before she could formulate an argument and decide to answer his proposal with a no, Lucas propelled her toward the back entrance.

Frustration welled that he hadn't been able to extract an answer from her *and* that he couldn't gauge her mood, but he kept a firm clamp on his temper. An edgy, hair-trigger temper that, until these past two weeks, he hadn't known existed.

He offered her his arm and forced himself to patience when she didn't immediately take it.

Clear, glacial-blue eyes clashed with his. "What makes you think I'm actually going to go through with this?"

Lucas noted that she stopped short of using the word *charade.* "I apologize for trying to bulldoze you," he said grimly. "I realize I've mishandled the situation."

He had used business tactics to try to maneuver Carla into an engagement. He had assumed that when he proposed marriage she would be, if not ecstatic, then, at least, happy.

Instead, she was decidedly *unhappy,* and now he was being left to sweat.

He acknowledged that he deserved it. If patience was now required to achieve a result, then he would be patient. "The ring is important. I need you to come inside and choose one."

"I suppose we need one because we've been *secretly engaged* for two years, so of course you would have loved me enough to buy a ring."

Ignoring Tiberio's scandalized expression, he unclenched his jaw. *"Esattamente,"* he muttered, momentarily forgetting his English. "If you don't have a ring, questions will be asked."

"So the ring is a prop, a detail that adds credence to the story."

The door popped open. A dapper gray-haired man, elegant in a dark suit and striped tie, appeared along with a security guard. "Mr. Atraeus," he murmured. "Ms. Ambrosi. My name is Carstairs, the store manager. Would you like to come this way?"

Keeping his temper firmly in check, Lucas concentrated on Carla. If she refused the ring, he would arrange for a selection to be sent to his apartment and she could choose one there. What was important was that she accept his proposal, and that hadn't happened yet. "Are you ready?"

Her eyes clashed with his again, but she took his arm.

Jaw clenched, Lucas controlled his emotions with a forcible effort. Fleetingly, he registered Tiberio's relief, an exaggerated expression of his own, as he walked up the steps and allowed Carla to precede him into the building.

She would say yes. She had to.

The turnaround was huge, but now that he had made the decision that he wanted her in his life permanently, he felt oddly settled.

Like it or not he was involved, his feelings raw, possessive. Sexually, he had lost control with Carla from the beginning, something that had never come close to happening with any other woman.

It was also a blunt fact that the thought of Carla with Panopoulos, or any man, was unacceptable. When he had walked into that particular wall, his reaction had cleared his mind. Despite everything that could go wrong with this relationship, Carla was his.

If he had to be patient and wait for her, then he would be patient.

Carla stepped into the room Carstairs indicated, glad for a respite from the odd intensity of Lucas's gaze and her own inner turmoil. For a fractured moment, she had been an inch away from giving up on the need to pressure some kind of admission out of Lucas and blurting out "yes." She would marry him, she would do whatever he wanted, if only he would keep on looking at her that way. But then the emotional shutters she had never been able to fathom had come crashing down and they had ended up stalemated again.

The room was an elegant private sitting room with sleek leather couches offset by an antique sideboard and coffee tables. Classical music played softly. The largest coffee table held a selection of rings nestled in black velvet trays.

Carstairs, who seemed to be staring at her oddly, indicated that she take a seat and view the rings, then asked if she would like coffee or champagne. Refusing either drink with a tight smile, she sat and tried to concentrate on the rings. Lucas, who had also refused a drink, paced the small room like an overlarge caged panther, then came to stand over her, distracting her further.

His breath stirred her hair as he leaned forward for a closer look. Utterly distracted by his closeness, she stared blindly at the rings, dazzled by the glitter but unable to concentrate, which was criminal because she loved pretty jewelry. "I didn't think you were interested in jewelry."

"I'm interested in you," he said flatly. "This one."

He picked out a pale blue pear-shaped stone, which she had noticed but bypassed because it occupied a tray that contained a very small number of exquisite rings, all with astronomical price tags.

He handed it to her then conferred briefly with Carstairs. "It's a blue diamond, from Brazil. Very rare, and the same color as your eyes. Do you like it?"

She studied the soft, mesmerizing glow of the diamond, but was more interested in the fact that he had picked the ring because it matched her eyes. She slipped the ring on her finger. Wouldn't you know, it was a perfect fit and it looked even better on. "I love it."

His gaze caught hers, held it, and for a moment she felt absurdly giddy.

"Then we'll take it." He passed Carstairs his credit card.

Yanking the ring off, she replaced it on its plush velvet tray and pushed to her feet, panic gripping her. "I haven't said yes yet."

Lucas said something in rapid Medinian to Carstairs. With a curt bow, the store manager, who could evidently speak the language, left the room, still with Lucas's card, which meant Lucas was buying the ring, regardless. Simultaneously, an elegant older woman in a simple black dress collected the remaining trays and made a swift exit along with Tiberio, leaving them alone. The blue ring, she noticed, was left on the coffee table.

In the background the classical music ended. Suddenly the silence was thick enough to cut.

Carla shoved to her feet and walked to the large bay window. She stared out into the tiny yard presently dominated by the limousine, and the issue she'd been desperate to ignore, which had hurt more than anything because it had cut into the most tender part of her, surfaced. As hard as she had tried for two years to be everything Lucas could want or need, it hadn't been enough. When the pressure had come on to commit, he hadn't wanted *her*. He had wanted Lilah, who in many ways was her complete opposite: calm, controlled and content to keep a low profile.

In retrospect, maybe she had tried too hard and he hadn't ever really seen her, just the glossy, upbeat side that was always "on." The one time he had truly seen her had been in Thailand. She had been too sick to try to be anything but herself, and he had run a mile. "What about Lilah?"

"I spoke to Lilah last night. Zane is taking care of her."

She met his gaze in the window. "I thought you were in love with her."

He came to stand behind her. "She was my date at the wedding, that was all. And, no, we didn't sleep together. We didn't kiss. I didn't so much as hold her hand."

Relief made Carla's legs feel as limp as noodles. He pulled her back against him in a loose hold, as the palm of one hand slid around to cup her abdomen.

"Marriage wasn't on my agenda, with anyone, but the situation has…changed. Don't forget it's entirely possible you're pregnant."

Lucas's hold tightened, making her intensely aware of his hard, muscled body so close behind her. Their reflection bounced back at her, Lucas large and powerfully male, herself paler and decidedly feminine. "I can't marry solely for a baby that might not exist! There has to be something more. Sienna is married to a man she loves. A man who loved her enough that he kidnapped her—"

"Are you saying you want to be *kidnapped?*"

She stared at the dark, irritable glitter of Lucas's eyes, the tough line of his jaw. Her own jaw set. "All I'm saying is that Constantine loves Sienna. It matters."

There was an arresting look in his eyes. "You love me."

Eleven

Carla inhaled sharply at the certainty in Lucas's voice, feeling absurdly vulnerable that, after two years of careful camouflage, she was so transparent now. She was also hurt by his matter-of-fact tone, as if her emotional attachment was simply a convenience that smoothed his path now. "What did you expect, that I was empty-headed enough that I was just having sex with you?"

"Meaning that was how I was with you?" His grip on her arms gentled. "Calm down. I didn't know until that moment. I'm…pleased."

"Because it makes things easier?"

"We're getting married," he said flatly. "This is not some business deal."

He didn't make the mistake of trying to kiss her. Instead he released her, walked over to the coffee table and picked the ring up.

The diamond shimmered in the light, impossibly beautiful, but it was the determined set to Lucas's jaw, the rock-solid patience in his gaze, that riveted her. "What if I'm not pregnant?"

"We'll deal with that possibility when we get to it."

Her jaw tightened. She didn't want to create difficulties, but neither could she let him put that ring on her finger without saying everything that needed to be said. "I'm not sure I want marriage under these conditions."

"That's your choice," he said flatly, his patience finally slipping. "But don't hold out for Alex Panopoulos to intervene. As of yesterday he has reviewed his options."

The sudden mention of Panopoulos was faintly shocking. "You warned him off."

"That's right." Lucas's voice was even, but his expression spoke volumes, coolly set with a primitive gleam in his eyes that sent a faint quiver zapping down her spine.

Just when she thought Lucas was cold and detached he proved her wrong by turning distinctly male and predatory.

It wasn't much, it wasn't enough, but it told her what she needed to know: Lucas was jealous. Given his cool, measured approach to every other aspect of his life, if he was jealous then he had to feel something powerful, something special, for her.

It was a leap in the dark. Marriage would be an incredible risk, but the past two years had been all about risk and she had already lost her heart. It came down to a simple choice. She could either walk away and hope to fall out of love with Lucas or she could stay and hold out for his love.

Her chin came up. When it came down to it she wasn't a coward. She would rather try and fail than not try at all.

"Okay," she said huskily, and extended her hand so he could slide the ring on her finger.

The fit was perfect. She stared at the fiery blue stone, her chest suddenly tight.

Lucas lifted her fingers to his lips. "It looks good."

The rough note in his voice, the unexpected caress, sent a shimmering wave of emotion through her. "It's beautiful."

He bent his head. Before she could react, he kissed her on the mouth. "I have good taste."

Despite her effort to stay calm and composed and not let Lucas see how much this meant to her, a wave of heat suffused her cheeks. "In rings or wives?"

He grinned quick and hard and dropped another quick kiss on her mouth. "Both."

Lucas shepherded Carla into the backseat of the limousine, satisfaction filling him at the sight of the ring glowing on her finger.

She loved him.

He had suspected it, but he hadn't known for sure until she had said the words. Her emotional involvement was an element he hadn't factored in when he had decided on marriage. He had simply formulated a strategy and kept to it until she had capitulated.

Now that he knew she loved him and had agreed to marry him, there would be no reason to delay moving her in with him. No reason to delay the wedding.

Marriage.

Since Sophie's death, marriage had not been an option, because he had never gotten past the fact that he still felt responsible for the accident.

It had taken a good year for the flashbacks of the accident to fade from his mind, another six months before he could sleep without waking up and reliving that night.

Sometimes, even now, he still woke up at night, reliving their last argument and trying to reinvent the past. He had avoided commitment for the simple reason that he knew his own nature: once he did commit he did so one hundred percent and he was fiercely protective. The night Sophie had died, he had been blindsided by the fact that she had aborted his child. He'd allowed her to throw her tantrum and leave. Maybe he was overcompensating now, but he would never allow himself, or any woman he was with, to be put in that situation again.

Until Carla, he had avoided becoming deeply involved with anyone. The week in Thailand had been a tipping point. Caring for Carla in that intimate situation had pushed him over an invisible boundary he had carefully skirted for five years. He hadn't liked the intense flood of emotion, or the implications for the future. He knew the way he was hard-wired. For as long as he could remember he had been the same: when it came to emotion it was all or nothing.

Now that Carla had agreed to marry him and it was possible that he would be a father, if not in the near future, then sometime over the next few years, he was faced with a double responsibility. He could feel the possessiveness, the desire to cushion and protect already settling in.

With Sophie he hadn't had time to absorb the impact of her pregnancy because it had been over before he had known about it. She hadn't given him a chance. With Carla the situation was entirely different. He knew that she would never abort their child. She would extend the same fiercely protective, single-minded love she gave her family to their baby.

Any child Carla had would be loved and pampered. Unlike Sophie, she would embrace the responsibility, the chills and the spills.

It was an odd moment to realize that one of the reasons he wanted to marry Carla was that he trusted her.

During the drive to the restaurant Lucas had booked, Carla wavered between staring with stunned amazement at the engagement ring and frantically wondering what Lucas's mother was going to think.

Like every other member of the Atraeus family, Maria Therese would know that Carla and Lucas had more than a hint of scandal in their past. Plus, the first and only time they had met, Lucas had been dating Lilah.

Lucas, who had been preoccupied with phone calls for the duration of the short trip to the restaurant, took her arm as she exited the limousine. "Now that we're engaged, there is one rule you will follow—don't talk to the press unless you've cleared it with me."

Carla stiffened. "PR is my job. I think I can handle the press."

Lucas nodded at Tomas, who was evidently waiting for them at the portico of the restaurant. "PR for Ambrosi is one thing. For the Atraeus family the situation is entirely different."

"I think I can be trusted."

His glance was impatient. "I know you can handle publicity. It's the security aspect that worries me. Every member of my family has to take care, and situations with the press provide prime opportunities for security breaches. If you're going to be talking to the press, a security detail needs to be organized. And by the way, I've booked you into the hotel for the launch party. We leave first thing in the morning."

Carla stopped dead in her tracks, a small fuzzy glow of happiness expanding in her chest. Lucas had obviously taken care of that detail before he had asked her to marry him, righting a wrong that had badly needed fixing. She knew she wouldn't be in charge of running the show, but that was a mere detail. She would still be able to make sure everything came off perfectly and that was what mattered. She was finally starting to believe that this marriage could work. "My contract as Ambrosi's public relations executive is up for renewal next week."

"It's as good as signed."

"That was almost too easy."

His arm slid around her waist, pulling her in against his side as they walked into the restaurant. "I was going to renew it anyway. You're damn good at the job, and besides, I want you to be happy."

Her happiness expanded another notch. It wasn't perfection yet—she still had to deal with that emotional distance thing that Lucas constantly pulled—but it was inching closer.

Maria Therese, Zane and Lilah were already seated at the table. Carla's stomach plunged as Lucas's mother gave her a measuring glance. With her smooth, ageless face and impeccable fashion sense, the matriarch of the Atraeus family had a reputation for being calm and composed under pressure. And with her late husband's affairs, there had been constant media pressure. "Does your mother know how long we've been involved?"

"You're an Ambrosi and my future wife. She'll be more than happy to accept you into the family."

Carla's stomach plunged. "Oh, good. She knows."

The resort chosen for the product launch was Balinese in style. Situated in its own private bay with heavy tropical gardens, it was also stunningly beautiful.

The hotel foyer was just as Carla remembered it when she had originally investigated the resort for the launch party. Constructed with all the grandeur of a movie set, it was both exotic and restful with a soaring atrium and tinkling fountains.

When Carla checked in at the front desk, however, she found that the guest room that had originally been booked for her had been canceled and there were no vacancies. Every room had been booked for the launch.

Lucas, casual in light-colored pants and a loose gauzy white shirt that accentuated his olive skin and made his shoulders look even broader, slipped his platinum card across the counter. "You're sharing with me. The suite's in my name."

So nice to be told. Even though she understood that Lucas was behaving this way because he was still unsure of her and he wanted to keep her close, there was no ignoring that it was controlling behavior. Pointedly ignoring the interruption, she addressed the receptionist. "Are you sure there are no rooms left? How about the room that was originally booked for Lilah Cole?"

Lilah had originally been slated to attend the launch. As the head designer she had a right to be there, but she had pulled out at the last minute.

The receptionist dragged her dazzled gaze off Lucas. "I'm sorry, ma'am, there was a waiting list. The room has already been allocated."

Carla waited until they were in the elevator. The feel-good mood of the two-hour drive from Sydney in Lucas's Ferrari was rapidly dissolving. Maybe it was a small point since they were engaged, but she would like to have been asked before Lucas decided she would be sharing his room. Lucas's controlling streak seemed to be growing by leaps and bounds and she was at a loss to understand why. She had agreed to marry him; life should be smoothing out, but it wasn't. Lucas was oddly silent, tense and brooding. Something was wrong and she couldn't figure out what it was.

Lucas leaned against the wall, arms folded over his chest, his gaze wary. "It's just a hotel room. I assumed you would want to share."

"I do."

Lucas frowned. The relaxed cast to his face, courtesy of an admittedly sublime night spent together in his bed, gone. "Then what's wrong? You already know that Lilah and I were not involved."

"It's not Lilah—"

The doors slid open. A young couple with three young children were waiting for the elevator.

Lucas propelled her out into the corridor. "We'll continue this discussion in our room."

Their luggage had already been delivered and was stacked to one side, but Carla barely registered that detail. The large airy room with its dark polished floors, teak furniture and soaring ceilings was filled with lush bouquets of roses in a range of hues from soft pinks to rich reds. Long stemmed and glorious, they overflowed dozens of vases, their scent filling the suite.

Dazed, she walked through to the bedroom, which was also smothered with flowers. An ice bucket of champagne and a basket crammed with fresh fruit and exquisitely presented chocolates resided on a small coffee table positioned between two chairs.

Lucas carried their bags into the bedroom. The second he set them down she flung her arms around him. "I'm sorry. You organized all this—it's beautiful, gorgeous—and all I could do was complain."

His arms closed around her, tucking her in snugly against him. The comfort of his muscled body against hers, the enticement of his clean scent, increased her dizzy pleasure.

The second she had seen what Lucas had done, how focused he was on pleasing her, the notion that there was something wrong had evaporated. Now she felt embarrassed and contrite for giving him such a hard time.

Carla spent a happy hour rearranging the flowers and unpacking. By the time she had finished laying out her dress for the evening function, Lucas had showered, changed into a suit and disappeared, called away to do a series of interviews.

A knock on the door made her frown. When she opened it a young woman in a hotel uniform was standing outside with a hotel porter. After a brief conversation she discovered that Lucas had arranged for the items to be delivered for her perusal. Anything she didn't want would be returned to the stores.

Feeling a bit like Alice falling down the rabbit hole, Carla opened the door wider so the porter could wheel in a clotheshorse that was hung with a number of plastic-shrouded gowns. At the base of the clotheshorse were boxes of shoes from the prominent design stores downstairs. She signed a docket and closed the door behind the hotel employees.

A quick survey of the gowns revealed that while they were all her size and by highly desirable designers, they were definitely not her style. Two had significantly high necklines, one a soft pink, the other an oyster lace. Both were elegant and gorgeously detailed, but neither conformed to her taste. The pink was too ruffled, like a flapper dress from the 1920s, and the oyster lace was stiffly formal and too much like a wedding gown.

The other boxes contained matching shoes and wraps and matching sets of silk underwear. She couldn't help noticing that none of the shoes had heels higher than two inches.

As dazzled as she was by the lavish gifts, nothing about any of them fitted her personality or style. Each item was decidedly conventional and, for want of a better word, boring, like something her mother would have worn.

Her pleasure in unwrapping the beautiful things was dissolving by the second. Aside from the underwear, which was sexy and beautiful, it was clear that Lucas had had one thought in mind when he had had the things sent up: he was trying to tone her down. That brought them back to the original problem. Despite the engagement, Lucas still didn't accept her for who she was. If he couldn't accept her, she didn't see how he could ever love her.

She found her phone and jabbed in the number of Lucas's new phone. He picked up on the second ring, his voice impatient.

She cut him off. "I'm not wearing any of these dresses you've just had sent up."

"Can we discuss this later?" The register of his voice was low, his tone guarded, indicating that he wasn't alone.

Carla was beyond caring. "I'm discussing it now. I resent the implication that I dress immodest—"

"When did I say—"

"I'm female and, newsflash, I have a *figure*. I do not buy clothes to emphasise sex appeal—"

"Wait there. I'm coming up."

A click sounded in her ear. Heart pounding, she snapped her phone closed, slipped it back in her bag and surveyed the expensive pile of items. Hurt squeezed her chest tight.

She had repacked the shoes and started on the underwear when the door opened.

Lucas snapped the door closed behind him and jerked at his tie. "What's the problem?"

Carla glanced away from the heated irritation in his gaze, his ruffled hair as if he'd dragged his fingers through it, and the sexy dishevelment of the loose tie.

She picked up the pink ruffled number. "This, for starters."

He frowned. "What's wrong with it?"

She draped the gown against her body. "Crimes against humanity. The fashion police will have me in cuffs before I get out of the elevator."

He pinched the bridge of his nose as if he was under intense pressure. "Do you realize that on Medinos, as your future husband I have the right to dictate what you wear?"

For a moment she thought he was joking. "That's *medieval*—"

"Maybe I'm a medieval kind of guy."

She blinked. She had been wanting to breach his inner barriers, but now she was no longer sure she was going to like what she'd find. The old Lucas had been a pussycat compared to what she was now uncovering. "I buy clothes because they make me look and feel good, not to showcase my breasts or any other part of my anatomy. If that means I occasionally flash a bit of cleavage, then you, and the rest of Medinos, are just going to have to adjust."

She snatched up the pink silk underwear, which in stark contrast to the dress was so skimpy it wouldn't keep a grasshopper warm. "Are these regulation?"

He hooked the delicate thong over one long brown finger. "Absolutely."

Carla snatched the thong back and tossed the pink underwear back in its box. Retrieving the list of items she had signed for, she did what she had been longing to do—ripped it into shreds and tossed the pieces at Lucas. The issue of clothing, as superficial as it seemed, ignited the deep hurt that Lucas still viewed her as his sexy, private mistress and not his future wife. "You can have your master plan back."

Lucas ignored the fluttering pieces of paper. "What master plan?"

"The one where you turn me into some kind of perfect stuffed mannequin and put me in a room on Medinos with one of those wooden embroidery frames in my hand."

Lucas rubbed the side of his jaw, his gaze back to wary. "Okay, I am now officially lost."

"I resent being treated as if I'm too dumb to know how I

should dress. This is not digging gold out of rocks or sweaty men building a hotel, this is a *fashion* industry event."

His jaw took on an inflexible look she was beginning to recognize. "We're engaged. Damned if I'm going to let other men ogle you."

She threw up her hands. "You're laying down the law, but you don't even know what I plan to wear tonight."

Marching to the bed, she held up a hanger that held a sleek gold sheath with a softly draped boat-shaped neckline. "It's simple, elegant, shows no cleavage—and, more to the point, I like it."

"In that case, I apologize."

Feeling oddly deflated, she replaced the dress on the bed. When she turned, Lucas pulled her into his arms.

Her palms automatically spread on his chest. She could feel the steady pound of his heart beneath the snowy linen of his shirt, the taut, sculpted muscle beneath. Her heart rate, already fast, sped up, but he didn't try to pull her closer or kiss her.

"It wasn't my intention to upset you, but there is one thing about me that you're going to have to understand—I don't share. When it comes down to it, I don't care what you wear. I just don't want other men thinking you're available. And from now on the press will watch you like a hawk."

"I'm not irresponsible, or a tease." She released herself from his hold. The problem was that she had never understood Lucas's mood swings; she didn't understand him. One minute he was with her, the next he was cut off and distant and she needed to know why, because that distance frightened her. Ultimately it meant it was entirely possible that one day he could close himself off completely and leave her.

She began carefully rehanging the dresses, needing something to do. "Why did you never want any kind of long-term relationship with me? You planned to finish with me all along."

He gripped his nape. "We met and went to bed on the same night. At that point marriage was not on my mind."

"And after Thailand it definitely wasn't."

"I compressed my schedule to be with you in Thailand. Taking further time off wasn't possible."

"What if I'd been *really* ill?"

His gaze flashed with impatience. "If you had been ill, you would have contacted me, but you didn't."

"No."

"Are you telling me you *were* ill and didn't contact me?" he asked quietly.

"Even if I was," she said, folding the oyster silk lingerie into the cloud of tissue paper that filled the box, "you didn't want to know because looking after me in Thailand was just a little too much reality for you, wasn't it?"

"Tell me more about how I was thinking," he muttered. "I'm interested to know just how callous you think I am."

Frustration pulling at her, she jammed the lid on the box. Lucas had cleverly turned the tables on her, but she refused to let up. It suddenly occurred to her that Lucas's behavior was reminiscent of her father's. Roberto Ambrosi had hated discussing personal issues. Every time anyone had probed him about anything remotely personal he had turned grouchy and changed the subject. Attack was generally seen as the most effective form of defense.

She realized now that every time she got close to what was bothering Lucas, he reacted like a bear with a sore head. If he was snapping now, she had to be close. "If I wasn't what you wanted before," she said steadily, "how can I be that person now?"

There was a small, vibrating silence. "Because I realized you weren't Sophie."

Carla froze. "Sophie Warrington?"

"That's right. We lived together for almost a year. She died in a car accident."

Carla blinked. She remembered the story. Sophie Warrington had been gorgeous and successful. She had also had a reputation for being incredibly spoiled and high maintenance. She had lost a couple of big contracts with cosmetic companies because she had thrown tantrums. She had also been famous for her affairs.

Suddenly, Carla's lack of control in the relationship made sense. She was dealing with a ghost—a gorgeous, irresponsible ghost who had messed Lucas around to the point that he had trouble trusting any woman.

Let alone one who not only looked like Sophie but who was caught up in the same glitzy world.

Twelve

Half an hour later, after taking her medication with a big glass of water, she nibbled on a small snack then decided to go for a walk along the beach and maybe have a swim before she changed for the evening function. It wouldn't exorcise the ghost of Sophie Warrington or her fear that Lucas might never trust enough to fall in love with her, but at least it would fill in time.

Winding her hair into a loose topknot, she changed into an electric blue bikini and knotted a turquoise sarong just above her breasts. After transferring her wallet to a matching turquoise beach bag, she slipped dark glasses on the bridge of her nose and she was good to go.

Half an hour later, she stopped at a small beach café, ordered a cool drink and glimpsed Tiberio loitering behind some palms. She had since found out that Tiberio wasn't just a bodyguard, he was Lucas's head of security. That being the case, the only logical reason for him to be here was that Lucas had sent him to keep an eye on her.

Annoyed that her few minutes of privacy had been invaded by security that Lucas hadn't had the courtesy to advise her about, she finished the drink and started back to the resort.

The quickest way was along the long, curving ocean beach, which was dotted with groups of bathers lying beneath bright beach umbrellas. As she walked, she stopped, ostensibly to pick up a shell, and glanced behind. Tiberio was a short distance back, making no attempt to conceal himself, a cell phone held to his ear.

No doubt he was talking to Lucas, reporting on her activities. Annoyed, she quickened her pace. She reached the resort gardens in record time but the fast walk in the humidity of late afternoon had made her uncomfortably hot and sticky. She strode past the cool temptation of a large gleaming pool. Making an abrupt turn off the wide path, she strode along a narrow winding bush walk with the intention of losing herself amongst the shady plantings.

Beneath the shadowy overhanging plants, paradoxically it was even hotter. Slowing down, she unwound her sarong and tied it around her waist for coolness and propped her dark glasses on top of her head.

Footsteps sounded behind her, coming fast. Annoyed, she spun, and came face-to-face with Alex Panopoulos.

Dressed in a pristine business suit, complete with briefcase, his smooth features were flushed and shiny with perspiration.

She frowned, perversely wondering what had happened to Tiberio, and suddenly uncomfortably aware of the brevity of her bikini top. "What are you doing here?"

Alex set his briefcase down and jerked at his edgily patterned tie. "I just arrived and was walking to my chalet when I saw you."

She frowned, disconcerted by the intensity of his expression and the fact that he had clearly run after her. "There was no need. I'll see you tonight at the presentation."

"No you won't. My invitation was rescinded."

"Lucas—"

"Yes," he muttered curtly, "which is why I wanted to talk with you privately."

His gaze drifted to her chest, making her fingers itch with the need to yank the sarong back up. "If it's about the job—"

"Not the job." He stepped forward with surprising speed and gripped her bare arms. This close the sharp scent of fresh sweat and cologne hit her full force.

His gaze centered on her mouth. "You must know how I feel about you."

"Uh, not really. Let me go." She tried to pull free. "I'm engaged to Lucas."

"Engagements can be ended."

A creepy sense of alarm feathered her spine. He wasn't letting go. She jerked back more strongly, but his grip tightened, drawing her closer.

The thought that he might try to kiss her made her stomach flip queasily. Alex had frequently made it clear that he was attracted to her, but she had dismissed his come-ons, aware that he also regularly targeted other women, including her sister, Sienna.

Deciding on strong action, she planted her palms on his chest but, before she could shove, Panopoulos flew backward, seemingly of his own accord. A split second later Lucas was towering over her like an avenging angel.

Alex straightened, his hands curling into fists.

Lucas said something low and flat in Medinian.

Alex flinched and staggered back another step, although Lucas hadn't either stepped toward him or touched him.

Flushing a deep red, Panopoulos lunged for his briefcase and stumbled back the way he'd come.

With fingers that shook slightly with reaction, Carla untied the sarong, dragged it back over her breasts and knotted it. "What did you say to him?"

Lucas's gaze glittered over her, coming to rest on the newly tied knot. "Nothing too complicated. He won't be bothering you again."

"Thank you. I was beginning to think he wasn't going to let go." Automatically, she rubbed at the red marks on her arms where Panopoulos had gripped her just a little too hard.

With gentle movements, Lucas pushed her hands aside so he could examine the marks. They probably wouldn't turn into bruises, but that didn't change the cold remoteness of his expression.

"Did he hurt you?"

"No." From the flat look in his dark eyes, the grim set to his jaw, Carla gained the distinct impression that if Panopoulos had stepped any further over the line than he had, Lucas wouldn't have been so lenient. A small tingling shiver rippled the length of her spine as she realized that Lucas was fiercely protective of her.

It was primitive, but she couldn't help the warm glow that formed because the man she had chosen as her mate was prepared to fight for her. In an odd way, Lucas springing to her defense balanced out the hurt of discovering how affected he'd been by Sophie Warrington. To the extent that his issues with her had permeated every aspect of his relationship with Carla.

His hand landed in the small of her back, the touch blatantly dominant and possessive, but she didn't protest. She was too busy wallowing in the happy knowledge that Lucas hadn't left it to Tiberio to save her. Instead, he had interrupted what she knew was a tight schedule of interviews and come after her himself. Despite the unpleasant shock of the encounter, she was suddenly glad that it had happened.

When they reached the room, Lucas kicked the door shut and leaned back against the gleaming mahogany and drew her close.

Carla, still on edge after the encounter, went gladly. Coiling her arms around his neck, she fitted her body against the familiar planes and angles of his, soaking in the calm reassurance of his no-holds-barred protection.

Tangling the fingers of one hand in her hair, Lucas tilted her head back and kissed her until she was breathless.

When he lifted his head, his expression was grim. "If you hadn't tried to get away from Tiberio, Panopoulos wouldn't have had the opportunity to corner you."

She felt her cheeks grow hot. "I needed some time alone."

"From now on, while we're at the hotel you either have security accompany you, or I do, and that's nonnegotiable."

"Yes."

He cupped her face, his expression bemused. "That was too easy. Why aren't you arguing?"

She smiled. "Because I'm happy."

A faint flush rimmed his taut cheekbones and suddenly she felt as giddy as a teenager.

"Damn, I wish I didn't have interviews." His mouth captured hers again.

She rose up into the kiss, angling her jaw to deepen it. This time the sensuality was blast-furnace hot, but she didn't mind. For the first time in over two years Lucas's kiss, his touch, felt absolutely and completely right.

He wanted her, but not just because he desired her. He wanted her because he *cared*.

* * *

Carla showered and dressed for the launch party. Lucas walked into the suite just as she was putting the finishing touches to her makeup.

"You're late." Pleasurable anticipation spiraled through her as he appeared behind her in the mirror, leaned down and kissed the side of her neck.

His gaze connected with hers in the mirror. "I had an urgent business matter to attend to."

And she had thrown his busy schedule off even further because he'd had to interrupt his meetings to rescue her.

The happy glow that had infused her when he'd read Panopoulos the riot act reignited, along with the aching knowledge that she loved him. It was on the tip of her tongue to tell him just how much when he turned and walked into the bathroom. Instead she called out, "I'll see you downstairs."

Minutes later, with Tiberio in conspicuous attendance, she strolled into the ballroom, which was already filled with elegantly gowned and suited clients, the party well under way.

She threaded her way through the crowd, accepting congratulations and fielding curious looks. When she walked backstage to check on the arrangements for the promotional show, Nina's expression was taut.

She threw Carla a harassed look. "A minor glitch. The model we hired is down with a virus, so the agency did the best they could at short notice and sent along a new girl." She jerked her head in the direction of the curtained-off area that was being used as dressing rooms.

Dragging the curtain back far enough so she could walk through, Carla stared in disbelief at the ultrathin model. She was the right height for the dress, but that was all. Obviously groomed for the runway, she was so thin that the gown, which had originally been custom-made for Carla, hung off her shoulders and sagged around her chest and hips.

Carla's assistant, Elise, was working frantically with pins. The only problem was, the dress—an aquamarine creation studded with hundreds of pearls in a swirling pattern that was supposed to represent the sea—could only be taken in at certain points.

To add insult to injury, the model was a redhead and nothing about the promotion was red. Everything was done in Ambrosi's signature aquamarine and pearl hues. The color mix was subtle, clean and classy, reflecting Ambrosi's focus on the luxury market.

"No," Carla said, snapping instantly into work mode, irritated by the imperfections of the model and the utter destruction of the promotion that had taken her long hours of painstaking time to formulate. "Take the pins out of the dress."

She smiled with professional warmth at the model and instructed her to change, informing her that she would be paid for the job and was welcome to stay the weekend at Ambrosi's expense, but that she wouldn't be part of the promotion that evening.

Clearly unhappy, the model shimmied out of the gown on the spot and walked, half-naked and stiff backed, into a changing cubicle. At that point, another curtain was swished wide, revealing the gaggle of young ballet girls, who were also part of the promotion, in various states of undress.

Tiberio made a strangled sound. Clearly unhappy that he had intruded into a woman's domain, he indicated he would wait in the ballroom.

Elise carefully shook out the gown, examined it for signs of damage and began pulling out the pins she'd inserted. "Now what?" She indicated her well-rounded figure. "If you think I'm getting into that dress, forget it."

"Not you. Me."

Nina looked horrified. "I thought the whole point of this was that you weren't to take part."

Carla picked up the elegant mask that went with the outfit and pressed it against her face. The mask left only her mouth and chin visible.

Her stomach tightened at the risk she was taking. "He won't know."

Thirteen

Carla stepped into the gown and eased the zipper up, with difficulty. The dress felt a little smaller and tighter than it had, because it had been taken in to fit the model who was off sick.

She fastened the exquisite trailing pearl choker, which, thankfully, filled most of her décolletage and dangled a single pearl drop in the swell of her cleavage.

Cleavage that seemed much more abundant now that the dress had been tightened.

She surveyed her appearance in the mirror, dismayed and a little embarrassed by the sensual effect of the too-tight dress.

Careful not to breathe too deeply and rip a seam, she fastened the webbed bracelet that matched the choker and put sexy dangling earrings in her lobes. She fitted the pearl-studded mask and surveyed the result in the mirror.

With any luck she would get through this without being

recognized. A few minutes on stage then she would make her exit and quickly change back into her gold dress and circulate.

Elise swished the curtain aside. "It's time to go. You're on."

Lucas checked his watch as he strolled through the ballroom, his gaze moving restlessly from face to face.

Tiberio had informed him that Carla was assisting the girls backstage with the small production they had planned. He had expected no less. When it came to detail, Carla was a stickler, but now he was starting to get worried. She should have been back in the ballroom, with him, by now.

He checked his watch again. At least Panopoulos was out of the picture. He had made certain of that.

Every muscle in his body locked tight as he remembered the frightened look on Carla's face as she'd tried to shove free of him. When he'd seen the marks on Carla's arms, he had regretted not hitting Panopoulos.

Instead, he had satisfied his need to drive home his message by personally delivering the older man to the airport and escorting him onto a privately chartered flight out.

Panopoulos had threatened court action. Lucas had invited him to try.

Frowning, he checked the room again. He thought he had seen Carla circulating when he had first entered the room, but the gold dress and dark hair had belonged to a young French woman. He was beginning to think that something else had gone wrong since the heart-stopping passion of those moments in their room and she had found something else to fret about.

The radiant glow on her face when he'd left her had hit him like a kick in the chest, transfixing him. He could remember her looking that way when they had first met, but gradually, over time, the glow had gone. He decided it was a grim testament to how badly he had mismanaged their relationship that Carla had ceased to be happy. From now on he was determined to do whatever it took to keep that glow in her eyes.

A waiter offered him a flute of champagne. He refused. At that moment there was a stir at one end of the room as Nina, who was the hostess for the evening, came out onto the small stage.

Lucas leaned against the bar and continued to survey the room as music swelled and the promotional show began. The room fell silent as the model, who was far more mouthwateringly sexy than he remembered, moved with smooth grace across the stage. *Floor show* wasn't the correct terminology for the presentation but he was inescapably driven to relabel the event.

Every man in the room was mesmerized, as the masked model, playing an ancient Medinian high priestess, moved through the simple routine, paying homage to God with the produce of the sea, a basket of Ambrosi pearls. With her long, elegant legs and tempting cleavage, she reminded him more of a Vegas dancer than any depiction of a Medinian priestess he had ever seen.

His loins warmed and his jaw tightened at his uncharacteristic loss of control. He had seen that dress on the model who was supposed to be doing the presentation. At that point the gown, which was largely transparent and designed so that pearl-encrusted waves concealed strategic parts and little else, had looked narrow and ascetically beautiful rather than sexy. He hadn't been even remotely turned-on.

The model turned, her hips swaying with a sudden sinuous familiarity as she walked, surrounded by a gaggle of young ballet dancers, all carrying baskets overflowing with free samples of Ambrosi products to distribute to clients.

Suspicion coalesced into certainty as his gaze dropped to the third finger of her left hand.

He swallowed a mouthful of champagne and calmly set the flute down. The mystery of his future wife's whereabouts had just been solved.

He had thought she was safely attired in the gold gown, minus any cleavage. Instead she had gone against his instructions and was busy putting on an X-rated display for an audience that contained at least seventy men.

Keeping a tight rein on his temper, he strode through the spellbound crowd and up onto the stage. Carla's startled gaze clashed with his. Avoiding a line of flimsy white pillars that were in danger of toppling, he took the basket of pearls she held, handed them to one of the young girls and swung her into his arms.

She clutched at his shoulders. "What do you think you're doing?"

Grimly, Lucas ignored the clapping and cheering as he strode off the stage and cut through the crowd to the nearest exit. "Removing you before you're recognized. Don't worry," he said grimly, "they'll think it's part of the floor show. The Atraeus Group's conquering CEO carrying off the glittering prize of Ambrosi Pearls."

"I can't believe you're romanticizing a business takeover, and it is *not* a floor show!"

He reached the elevator and hit the call button with his elbow, his gaze skimmed the enticing display of cleavage. "What happened to the model I employed?"

"She came down with a virus. The replacement they sent didn't fit the dress. If I hadn't stepped in, the only option would have been to cancel the promotion."

A virus. That word was beginning to haunt him. "And canceling would have been such a bad idea?"

"Our events drive a lot of sales. Besides, I'm wearing a mask. No one knew."

"*I* knew."

She ripped off the mask, her blue gaze shooting fire. "I don't see how."

He took in the sultry display of honey-tanned skin. Cancel the Vegas dancer. She looked like an extremely expensive courtesan, festooned with pearls. *His* courtesan.

It didn't seem to matter what she wore, he reflected. The clothing could look like a sack on any other woman, but on Carla it became enticingly, distractingly sexy. "Next time remember to take off the engagement ring."

The elevator doors opened. Seconds later they had reached their floor. Less than a minute later Lucas kicked the door to their suite closed.

"You realize I need to go back to the party."

He set her down. "Just not in that dress."

"Not a problem, it's not my color." Carla tugged at the snug fit of the dress. Fake pearls pinged on the floor. A seam had given way while Lucas was carrying her, but on the positive side, at least she could breathe now. She eyed Lucas warily. "What do you think you're doing?"

He had draped his suit jacket over the back of a couch, loosened his tie and strolled over to the small business desk in the corner of the sitting room. She watched as he flipped his laptop open. "Checking email."

The abrupt switch from scorching possessiveness to cool neutrality made her go still inside. She had seen him do this often. In the past, usually, just before he would leave her apartment he would begin immersing himself in work— phone calls, emails, reading documents. She guessed that on some level she had recognized the process for what it was; she just hadn't ever bothered to label it. Work was his coping mechanism, an instant emotional off button. She should know. She had used it herself often enough.

She watched as he scrolled through an email, annoyed at the way he had switched from blazing hot to icy cool. Lucas had removed her from the launch party with all the finesse of a caveman dragging his prize back to the fire. He had gotten his way; now he was ignoring her.

The sensible option would be to get out of the goddess outfit, put on another dress and go downstairs and circulate before finding her gold dress and handbag, which she had left backstage. But that was before her good old type A personality decided to make a late comeback.

Ever since she had been five years old on her first day at school and her teacher, Mrs. Hislop, had put daddy's little girl in the back row of the classroom, she had understood one defining fact about herself: she did not like being ignored.

Walking to the kitchenette, she opened cupboards until she found a bowl. She needed to eat. Cereal wasn't her snack of choice this late, but it was here, and the whole point was that she stayed in the suite with Lucas until he realized that she was not prepared to be ignored.

She found a minipacket of cereal, emptied it into the bowl then tossed the packaging into the trash can, which was tucked into a little alcove under the bench.

Lucas sent her a frowning glance, as if she was messing with his concentration. "I thought you were going to change and get back to the party."

She opened the fridge and extracted a carton of milk. "Why?"

"The room is full of press and clients."

She gave him a faintly bewildered look, as if she didn't understand what he was talking about, but inwardly she was taking notes. He clearly thought she was a second Sophie, a party girl who loved to be the center of attention. "Nina and Elise are taking care of business. I don't need to be there."

"It didn't look that way ten minutes ago."

She shrugged. "That was an emergency."

Aware that she now had Lucas's attention, she opened the carton with painstaking precision and poured milk over the cereal. Grabbing a spoon, she strolled out into the lounge, sat on the sofa and turned the TV on. She flicked through the channels till she found a talk show she usually enjoyed.

Lucas took the remote and turned the TV off. "What are you up to?"

Carla munched on a spoonful of cereal and stared at the now blank screen. Before the party she had found reasons to adore Lucas's dictatorial behavior. Now she was back to loathing it, but she refused to allow her annoyance to show. She had wanted Lucas's attention and now she had gotten it. "Considering my future employment. I'm not good with overbearing men."

"You are not going to work for Panopoulos."

She ate another mouthful of cereal. He was jealous; she was getting somewhere. "I guess not, since I have an iron-clad contract I signed only yesterday."

Lucas tossed the remote down on the couch and dispensed with his tie. "Damn. You must be sleeping with the boss."

"Plus, I have shares."

"It's not a pleasing feminine trait to parade your victories." He took the cereal bowl from her and set it down on the coffee table. Threading her fingers with his, he pulled her to her feet.

More pearls pinged off the dress as she straightened. A tiny tearing sound signaled that another seam had given. "You shouldn't take food from a woman who could be pregnant."

His gaze was arrested. "Do you think you are?"

"I don't know yet." She had left the test kit behind. With everything that had happened, taking time out to read the instructions and do the test hadn't been a priority.

"I could get used to the idea." Cupping her face, he dipped his head and touched his mouth to hers.

The soft, seducing intimacy of the kiss made Carla forget the next move in her strategy. Before she could edit her response, her arms coiled around his neck. He made a low sound of satisfaction, then deepened the kiss.

Hands loosely cupping her hips, he walked her backward, kiss by drugging kiss, until they reached the bedroom. She felt a tug as the zipper on the dress peeled down, then a loosening at the bodice. More pearls scattered as he pulled the dress up and over her head and tossed it on the floor.

"The dress is ruined." Not that she really cared. It had only been a prop and it had served its purpose, in more ways than one.

"Good. That means you can't wear it again."

Stepping out of her heels, she climbed into bed and pulled the silk coverlet over her as she watched him undress. With his jet-black hair and broad, tanned shoulders he looked sleek and muscular.

The bed depressed as he came back down beside her. The clean scent of his skin made her stomach clench.

He surveyed the silk coverlet with dissatisfaction. "This needs to go." He dragged it aside as he came down on the bed. One long finger stroked over the pearl choker at her throat down to the single dangling pearl nestled in the shadowy hollow between her breasts. "But you can keep this on."

She had forgotten about the jewelry. Annoyed by the suggestion, which seemed more suited to a mistress than a future wife, she scooted over on the bed, wrapping the coverlet around her as she went. "You just destroyed an expensive gown. If you think I'm going to let you make love to me while I'm wearing an Ambrosi designer orig—"

His arm curled around her waist, easily anchoring her to the bed. "I'll approve the write-off for it."

Despite her reservations, unwilling excitement quivered through her as he loomed over her, but he made no effort to do anything more than keep her loosely caged beneath him.

"Whether we make love or not," he said quietly, "is your decision, but before you storm off, you need to know that I've organized a special license on Medinos. We're going to be married before the week is out."

"You might need my permission for that."

Something flared in his gaze and she realized she had pushed him a little too hard. "Not on Medinos."

"As I recall from Sienna's wedding, I still have to say yes."

Frustration flickered in his gaze and then she finally got him. For two years she had been focused on organizing their time together, taking care of every detail so that everything was as perfect as she could make it, given their imperfect circumstances. Lucas had fallen in with her plans, but she had overlooked a glaring, basic fact. Lucas was male; he needed to be in control. He now wanted her to follow the plan he had formulated, and she was frustrating him.

He cupped her face. "I have the special license. I don't care where we get married, just as long as it happens. Damned if I want Panopoulos, or any man, thinking you're available."

Unwilling delight filtered through the outrage that had driven her ever since she had realized that Lucas had developed a coping mechanism for shutting her out. The incident with Alex seemed a lifetime away, but it had only been hours.

She understood that in Lucas's mind he had rescued her for a second time that day, this time from a room full of men. As domineering and abrasive as his behavior was, in an odd way, it was the assurance she so badly needed that he cared. After watching him detach and walk away from her for more than two years, she wasn't going to freeze him out just when she finally had proof that he was falling for her.

"Yes."

His gaze reflected the same startled bemusement she had glimpsed that afternoon. "That's settled, then."

Warmth flared to life inside her. The happy glow expanded when he touched his lips to hers, the soft kiss soothing away the stress of dealing with Lucas's dictatorial manner. Sliding her fingers into the black silk of his hair, she pulled him back for a second kiss, then a third, breathing in his heat and scent. The kiss deepened, lingered. The silk coverlet slid away and she went into his arms gladly.

Sometime later, she woke when Lucas left the bed and walked to the bathroom, blinking at the golden glow that still flooded the room from the bedside lamp. Chilled without his body heat, she curled on her side and dragged the coverlet up high around her chin.

The bed depressed as Lucas rejoined her. One arm curled around her hips, he pulled her back snug against him. His palm cupped her abdomen, as if he was unconsciously cradling their baby.

Wistfully, her hand slipped over his, her fingers intertwining as she relaxed back into the blissful heat of his body. She took a moment to fantasize about the possibility that right at that very moment there could be an embryo growing inside her, that in a few months they would no longer be a couple, they would be a family. "Do you think we'll make good parents?"

"We've got every chance."

She twisted around in his grip, curious about the bitter note in his voice. "What's wrong?"

He propped himself on one elbow. "I had a girlfriend who was pregnant once. She had an abortion."

"Sophie Warrington?"

"That's right."

"You told me about her. She died in a car accident."

There was silence for a long, drawn-out moment. "Sophie had an abortion the day before she died. When she finally got around to telling me that she'd aborted our child before even telling me she was pregnant, we had a blazing argument. We broke up and she drove away in her sports car. An hour later she was dead."

Carla blinked. She hadn't realized that Lucas had split with Sophie before she had died. She smoothed her palm over his chest. "I'm sorry. You must have loved her."

"It was an addiction more than love."

Something clicked into place in her mind. Lucas had once used that term with regard to her. She hadn't liked it at the time, because it implied an unwilling attraction. "You don't see me as another Sophie?"

His hand trapped hers, holding it pressed against his chest so she could feel the steady thud of his heart. "You are similar in some ways, but maybe that's how the basic chemistry works. Both you and Sophie are my type."

Her stomach plunged a little. There it was again, the unwilling element to the attraction.

She knew he hadn't considered her marriageable in the beginning, because in his mind marriage hadn't fitted with the addictive sexual passion she had inspired in him. Admittedly, she hadn't helped matters. She had been busy trying to de-stress in line with her doctor's orders and keep their relationship casual but organized until the problems between both families had been rectified. In the process she had given him a false impression of her values. He had gotten to know who she really was a little better in the past few days, but that was cold comfort when she needed him to love her.

Fear spiked though her at the niggling thought that, if he

categorized her as being like Sophie, it was entirely possible that he wouldn't fall in love with her, that he would always see her as a fatal attraction and not his ideal marriage partner.

If she carried that thought through to its logical conclusion, it was highly likely that once the desire faded, he would fall for the kind of woman that in his heart he really wanted. "What happens when I get old, or put on weight, or…get sick?"

Physical attraction would fade fast and then where would they be?

She cupped his jaw. "I think I need to know *why* you can't resist me, because if what you feel is only based on physical attraction, it won't last."

He stoked a finger down the delicate line of her throat to her collarbone. "It's chemistry. A mixture of personality and the physical."

She frowned, her dissatisfaction increasing. "If you feel this way about me then how could you have been attracted to Lilah?"

As soon as she said Lilah's name, she wished she hadn't. Despite having Lucas's ring on her finger, she couldn't forget the weeks of stress when Lucas had avoided her then the sudden, hurtful way he had replaced her with Lilah.

"If you're jealous of Lilah, you don't need to be."

"Why?" But the question was suddenly unnecessary, because the final piece of the puzzle had just dropped into place. Lucas hadn't wanted Lilah for the simple reason that he had barely had time to get to know her. She had been part of a coldly logical strategy. An instant girlfriend selected for the purpose of spelling out in no uncertain terms that his relationship with Carla was over.

Fourteen

Carla stiffened. All the comments he'd made about her not needing to worry about Lilah and the quick way he had ended his relationship with her suddenly made perfect sense. "I have no reason to be jealous of Lilah, because you were never attracted to her."

His abrupt stillness and his lack of protest were damning.

"You manufactured a girlfriend." Her throat was tight, her voice husky. "You picked out someone safe to take to the wedding to make it easy to break up with me. You knew that if I thought you had fallen for another woman I would keep my distance and not make a fuss."

He loomed over her, his shoulders blocking out the dim glow from the lamp. "Carla—"

"No." Pushing free of his arms, she stumbled out of bed and struggled into her robe.

She yanked the sash tight as another thought occurred, giving her fresh insight into just how ruthless and serpentine

Lucas had been. "And you didn't pick just anyone to play your girlfriend. You were clever enough to select someone from Ambrosi Pearls, so the relationship covered all bases and would be in my face at work. That made it doubly clear to me that you were off-limits. It also made it look like you wanted her close, that you couldn't bear to have her out of your sight."

The complete opposite of his treatment of her.

Through the course of their relationship she had been separated and isolated from almost every aspect of his personal and business life.

Suddenly the room, with its romantic flowers, her clothes and jewelry draped over furniture and on the floor, emphasized how stupid she had been. Lucas's silence wasn't making her feel any better. "You probably even wanted to push me into leaving Ambrosi, which would get me completely out of your hair."

He shoved off the bed, found his pants and pulled them on. "I had no intention of depriving you of your job."

She stared at him bleakly, uncaring about that minor detail, when his major sin had been his complete and utter disregard for her feelings and her love. "What incentive did you offer Lilah to pose as your girlfriend?"

"I didn't pay Lilah. She knew nothing about this beyond the fact that I asked her to be my date at Constantine's wedding. That was our first, and last, date."

He caught her around the waist and pulled her close. "Do you believe me?"

She blinked. "Do you love me?"

There was the briefest of hesitations. "You know I do."

She searched his expression. It was a definite breakthrough, but it wasn't what she needed, not after the stinging hurt of finding out that he had used Lilah to facilitate getting rid of her.

His gaze seared into hers. "I'm sorry."

He bent and kissed her and the plunging disappointment receded a little. He was sorry and he very definitely wanted her. Maybe he even did love her. It wasn't the fairy tale she had dreamed about, but it was a start.

A few days ago she had been desperate for just this kind of chance with Lucas. Now too she was possibly pregnant. She owed it to herself and to Lucas to give him one more chance.

After an early breakfast, Carla strolled into the conference room Ambrosi had booked for its sales display. Lucas had phone calls to make in their suite, then meetings with buyers. Carla had decided to make herself useful and help Elise put together the jewelry display and set out the sales materials and press kits.

The fact that, if Lilah had been here, setting up the jewelry would have been her job was a reminder she didn't need, but she had to be pragmatic. Lilah was likely to be a part of the landscape for the foreseeable future, and she probably wasn't any happier about the situation than Carla. They would both have to adjust.

Security was already in place and lavish floral displays filled the room with the rich scent of roses. Elise had arranged for Ambrosi's special display cases to be positioned around the room. All that remained was for the jewelry, which was stored in locked cases, to be set out and labeled.

Elise, already looking nervous and ruffled, handed her a clipboard. "Just to make things more complicated, last night Lilah won a prestigious design award in Milan for some Ambrosi pieces. The buzz is *huge*." She snapped a rubber band off a large laminated poster. "Lucas had this expressed from the office late last night." She unrolled the poster, which was a blown-up publicity shot of Lilah, looking ultrasleek and gorgeous in a slim-fitting white suit, Ambrosi pearls at her lobes and her throat. With the pose she had struck and her calm gaze square on to the camera, Carla couldn't help thinking she looked eerily like the Atraeus bride in the portrait both she and Zane had studied at the prewedding dinner.

Elise glanced around the room. "I think I'll put it there, so people will see it as soon as they walk into the room. What do you think?"

Carla stared at the background of the poster. If she wasn't mistaken Lilah's image was superimposed over a scenic shot of Medinos—probably taken from one of the balconies of the *castello*. It was a small point, but it mattered. "Lucas ordered that to be done *late* last night?"

If that was the case, the only window of time he'd had was the few minutes after he had abducted her from the party when he had suddenly lost all interest in her because he had been so absorbed with what he was doing online.

Ordering a poster of the gorgeous, perfect Lilah.

Elise suddenly looked uncertain. "Uh, I think so. That's what he said."

Carla smiled and held out her hand. "Cool. Give the poster to me."

Elise went a little pale, but she handed the poster over.

Carla studied the larger-than-life photo. Her first impulse was to fling it into the ocean so she didn't have to deal with all that perfection. With her luck, the tide would keep tossing the poster back.

"I need scissors."

Elise found a pair and handed them over. Carla spent a happy few minutes systematically reducing the poster to an untidy pile of very small pieces.

Elise's eyes tracked the movement as Carla set the scissors down. She cleared her throat. "Do you want to sort through the jewelry, or would you prefer I did that?"

"I'm here to help. I'll do it."

"Great! I'll do the press kits." She dug in her briefcase. "Here's the plan for the display items. With all of the other publicity about, uh, Lilah, our sales have gone through the roof. We've already received orders from some of the attending clients so some of that jewelry is for clients and not for display. With any luck, they've kept the orders separate."

Carla slowly relaxed, determinedly thinking positive thoughts as she checked off the orders against the packing slip and set those packages to one side. Her mood improved by the second as she began putting the display together, anchoring the gorgeous, intricate pieces securely on black velvet beds then locking the glass cases. Lilah may have designed most of the jewelry, but they were Ambrosi pieces and she was proud of them. She refused to allow any unhappiness she felt about Lilah affect her pride in the family business.

A courier arrived with a package. Elise signed for it, shrugging. "This is weird. All the rest was delivered yesterday."

Carla took the package and frowned. The same courier firm had delivered it, but this one wasn't from the Ambrosi warehouse in Sydney. The package had been sent by another jeweler, the same Atraeus-owned company from which Lucas had purchased her engagement ring. That meant that whatever the package contained it couldn't be either an order for a customer or jewels for the launch.

Anticipation and a glow of happy warmth spread through her as she studied the package. She had her ring, which meant Lucas must have bought her something else, possibly a matching pendant or bracelet.

Her heart beat a little faster. Perhaps even matching wedding rings.

The temptation to open the package was almost overwhelming, but she managed to control herself. Lucas had bought her a gift, his first real gift of love, without pressure or prompting. She wasn't about to spoil his moment when he gave her the special piece he had selected.

She studied the ring on her finger, unable to contain her pleasure. She didn't care about the size of the diamond or the cost. What mattered was that Lucas had chosen it because it matched her eyes. Every time she looked at the ring she remembered that tiny, very personal, very important detail. It was a sign that he was one step closer to truly loving and appreciating her. After what had happened last night, how close they had come to splitting up again, she treasured every little thing that would help keep them together.

Elise finished shoving boxes and Bubble Wrap in the bin liner the hotel had provided. She waggled her brows at the package. "Not part of the display, huh? Looks interesting. Want me to take it to Lucas? I'm supposed to take the Japanese client he's meeting with to the airport in about ten minutes."

"Hands off." Carla's fingers tightened on the package. Despite knowing that Elise was teasing her, she felt ridiculously possessive of whatever Lucas had bought for her.

A split second later, Lucas strolled into the conference room. Immediately behind him, hotel attendants were setting up for morning tea, draping the long tables in white tablecloths and setting out pastries and finger food. Outside, in the lobby, she could hear the growing chatter. Any minute now, buyers and clients would start pouring into the conference room and there would be no privacy. The impulse to thrust the package at Lucas and get him to open it then and there died a death.

Lucas's gaze locked with hers then dropped to the glossy cut-up pieces of poster still strewn across the table. He lifted a brow. "What's that?"

"Your poster of Lilah."

There was a moment of assessing silence.

Lucas was oddly watchful, recognizing and logging the changes in her. As if he was finally getting that she was a whole lot more than the amenable, compartmentalized lover he had spent the past two years holding at a distance.

In that moment Carla knew Lilah had to go completely, no matter how crucial she was to Ambrosi Pearls. If she and Lucas were to have a chance at a successful marriage, they couldn't afford a third person in the equation.

Lucas lifted a brow. "What's in the package?"

"Nothing that won't keep." She pushed the package out of sight in her handbag then briskly swept all the poster fragments into the trash.

Whatever Lucas had bought her, she couldn't enjoy receiving it right at that minute, not with the larger-than-life specter of Lilah still hanging over them.

The weekend finished with a dinner cruise, by the end of which Lucas was fed up with designer anything. Give him steel girders and mining machinery any day. Anything but the shallow, too bright social whirl that was part and parcel of the world of luxury retailing.

He kept his arm around Carla's waist as they stood on the quay, bidding farewell to the final guests.

Carla was exhausted—he could feel it in the way she leaned into him—and her paleness worried him. The last thing she needed was another viral relapse.

He had insisted she fit in a nap after lunch. It had been a struggle to make her let go of the organizational reins, but in the end he had simply picked her up and carried her to their room. He had discovered that there was something about the masculine, take-charge act of picking Carla up that seemed to reach her in a way that words couldn't.

She had been oddly quiet all day, but he had expected that. He had made a mistake with the poster. The second he had walked into the conference room that morning and seen the look on Carla's face he had realized just how badly he had messed up. He had grimly resolved to take more care in future.

Her quietness had carried over into the evening. He had debated having her stay in their suite and rest, but in the end he had allowed her to come on the cruise for one simple reason. If he left her behind, she might not be there when he returned.

Lucas recognized Alan Harrison, a London buyer and the last straggling guest.

He paused to shake Lucas's hand. "Lilah Cole, the name on everyone's lips. You might have trouble holding on to her now, Atraeus. I know Catalano jewelry in Milan is impressed with her work. Wouldn't be surprised if they try and spirit her away from you."

Lucas clenched his jaw as Carla stiffened beside him. "That won't happen for at least two years. Lilah just signed a contract to take on the Medinos retail outlet as well as head up the design team."

"Medinos, huh? Smart move. Pretty girl, and focused. Got her in the nick of time. Another few days and you would have lost her."

Carla waited until Harrison had gone then gently detached herself from his hold. "You didn't tell me you had renewed Lilah's contract."

There was no accusation in her voice, just an empty neutrality, but Lucas had finally learned to read between the lines. When Carla went blank that was when she was feeling the most, and when *he* was being weighed in the balance.

Two years, and he hadn't understood that one crucially important fact. "I offered her the Medinos job a couple of days ago. If I'd realized how much it would hurt you I would have let her go. At the time removing her to Medinos for two years seemed workable, since I'll be running the Sydney office for the foreseeable future and we'll be based here."

"You did that for me." There was a small, vibrating silence and he was finally rewarded with a brilliant smile. "Thank you."

"You're welcome." Grinning, he pulled her into his arms.

Carla slipped out of her heels as she walked into their suite. Her feet were aching but she was so happy she hardly noticed the discomfort.

Lucas had finally crossed the invisible line she had needed him to cross; he had committed himself to her, and the blood was literally fizzing through her veins.

Maybe she should have felt this way when they had gotten engaged, but the reality was that all he'd had to do was say words and buy a ring. As badly as she had wanted to, she hadn't felt secure. Now, for the first time in over two years, she finally did.

The fact that he had arranged for Lilah to work in Medinos because they would be based in Sydney for two years had been the tipping point.

He had made an arrangement to ensure their happiness. He had used the word *they*. It was a little word, but it shouted commitment and togetherness.

Two years in Sydney. Together.

Taking Lucas by the hand, she pulled him into the bedroom, determinedly keeping her gaze away from the bedside bureau where she had concealed the package that had arrived that morning. "Sit down." She patted the bed. "I'll get the champagne."

He shrugged out of his jacket and tossed it over a chair before jerking at his tie. "Maybe you shouldn't drink champagne."

"Sparkling water for me, champagne for you."

"What are we celebrating, exactly?"

"You'll see in a minute."

He paused in the act of unbuttoning his shirt. "You're pregnant."

The hope in Lucas's voice sent a further shiver of excitement through her. Not only did he want her enough that he had bought her a wonderful surprise gift, he really did want their baby. Suddenly, after weeks, years, of uncertainty everything was taking on the happy-ever-after fairy tale sparkle she had always secretly wanted.

Humming to herself, she walked into the kitchen and opened a chilled bottle of vintage French champagne. The label was one of the best. The cost would be astronomical, but this was a special moment. She wanted every detail to be perfect. She put the champagne and two flutes on a tray and added a bottle of sparkling water for herself. On the way to the bedroom, she added a gorgeous pink tea rose from one of the displays.

She set the tray down on the bedside table as Lucas padded barefoot out of the bathroom. In the dim lamp-lit room with his torso bare, his dark dress trousers clinging low on narrow hips, his bronzed, muscular beauty struck her anew and she was suddenly overwhelmed by emotion and a little tearful.

Lucas cupped her shoulders and drew her close. "What's wrong?"

She snuggled against him, burying her face in the deliciously warm, comforting curve of his shoulder. "Nothing, except that I love you."

There was a brief hesitation, then he drew her close. "And I love you."

Carla stiffened at the neutral tone of his voice then made an effort to dismiss the twinge of disappointment that, even now, with this new intimacy between them, Lucas still couldn't relax into loving her.

She pushed away slightly, enough that she could see his face and read his expression, but she was too late to catch whatever truth had been in his eyes when he had said those three little words.

Forcing a bright smile, she released herself from Lucas's light hold, determined to recapture the soft, fuzzy fairy-tale glow. "Time for the champagne."

Lucas took the bottle from her and set it back down on the tray.

He reeled her in close. "I don't need a drink."

His head dipped, his lips brushed hers. She wound her arms around his neck, surrendering to the kiss as he pulled her onto the bed. Long seconds later he propped his head on one elbow and wound a finger in a coiling strand of her hair. "What's wrong? You're like a cat on hot bricks."

Rolling over, Carla opened the bureau drawer and took out the courier package. "This came today."

The heavy plastic rustled as she handed it to Lucas. Instead of the teasing grin she had expected, Lucas's gaze rested on the courier package and he went curiously still.

A sudden suspicion gripped her.

Clambering off the bed she took the package and ripped at the heavy plastic.

"Carla—"

"No. Don't talk." Tension banded her chest as she walked out to the kitchen, found a steak knife in the drawer and slit the plastic open. A heavy, midnight-blue box, tied with a black silk bow, the jeweler's signature packaging, tumbled out of layers of Bubble Wrap onto the kitchen counter.

Not an oblong case that might hold a necklace, or a bracelet. A ring box.

Lucas loomed over her as she tore the bow off. Maybe

it was a set of wedding rings. Lucas wanted an early wedding. It made sense to order the rings from the same place they had bought her engagement ring.

"Carla—"

She already knew. Not wedding rings. She flipped the jewelry case open.

A diamond solitaire glittered with a soft, pure fire against midnight-blue velvet.

Fingers shaking, she slid the ring onto the third finger of her right hand. It was a couple of sizes too small and failed to clear her knuckle. The bright, illusory world she had been living in dissolved.

The ring had never been meant for her. The elegant, classic engagement ring had been selected and sized with someone else in mind.

Lilah.

Fifteen

Carla replaced the ring in its box and met Lucas's somber gaze head-on. "You weren't just dating Lilah to facilitate making a clean break with me, were you? You intended to marry her."

Lucas's expression was calmly, coolly neutral. "I had planned to propose marriage, but that was before—"

"Why would you want to marry Lilah when you still wanted me?" She couldn't say *love,* because she now doubted that love had ever factored in. Lucas had wanted her, period. He had felt desire, passion: lust.

"It was a practical decision."

"Because otherwise you were worried that when Constantine and Sienna tied the knot you might be pressured into marrying me."

Impatience flashed in his gaze. "No one could pressure me into marriage. I wanted you. I would have married you in a New York second."

Realization dawned. "Then lived to regret it."

"I didn't think what we had would last."

"So you tied yourself into an arrangement with Lilah so you couldn't be tempted into making a bad decision."

His brows jerked together. "There was no 'arrangement.' All Lilah knew was that I wanted to date her."

"With a view to marriage."

"Yes."

Because she wouldn't have gone out with him otherwise. Certainly not halfway across the world to a very public family wedding.

Hurt spiraled through her that Lucas hadn't bothered to refute her statement that marrying her would have been a bad decision. And that he had so quickly offered Lilah what she had longed for and needed from him.

Throat tight, eyes stinging, Carla snapped the ring box closed and jammed it back into the courier bag. She suddenly remembered the odd behavior of the manager of Moore's. It hadn't been because their engagement was so sudden, or because of the scandal in the morning paper. The odd atmosphere had been because Lucas had bought *two* engagement rings in the same week for two separate women.

Blindly, she shoved the courier bag at Lucas. "You were going to propose to her *here,* at this product launch." Why else would he have requested the ring be couriered to the hotel?

Carla remembered the flashes of sympathy in Lilah's gaze on Medinos, her bone-white face outside of Lucas's apartment when the reporter had snapped Carla and Lucas kissing. Lilah had expected more than just a series of dates. She wouldn't have been with Lucas otherwise.

"You were never even remotely in love with Lilah."

"No."

Her head jerked up. "Then, why consider marriage?"

His expression was taut. "The absence of emotion worked for me. I wasn't after the highs and lows. I wanted the opposite."

"Because of Sophie Warrington."

"That's right," he said flatly. "Sophie liked bright lights, publicity. She loved notoriety. We clashed constantly. The night of the crash we argued and she stormed out. That was the last time I saw her alive. I shouldn't have let her go, should have stopped her—"

"If she wasn't your kind of girl, why were you with her?"

"Good question," he said grimly. "Because I was stupid enough to fall for her. We were a mismatch. We should never have been together in the first place."

Carla's jaw tightened. "You do still think I'm like her," she said quietly. "Another Sophie."

His expression was closed. "I…did."

The hesitation was the final nail in the proverbial coffin. Her stomach plummeted. "You still do."

"I've made mistakes, but I know what I want," Lucas said roughly.

"Me, or the baby I might possibly be having?" Because if Lucas still didn't know who she was as a person, the baby seemed the strongest reason for marriage. And she couldn't marry someone who saw his attraction to her as a weakness, a character flaw. She stared blankly around the flower-festooned room. "If you don't mind, I'd like to get some sleep."

Stepping past Lucas, she walked into the bedroom and grabbed a spare pillow and blanket from the closet.

"Where are you going?"

"To sleep on the couch."

"That's not necessary. I'll take the couch."

She flinched at the sheer masculine beauty of his broad shoulders and muscled chest. She had fallen in love with a mirage, she thought bleakly, a beautiful man who was prepared to care for her but who, ultimately, had never truly wanted to be in love with her. "No. Right now I really would prefer the couch."

His fingers curled around her upper arms. "We can work this through. I can explain—"

She went rigid in his grip. The pillow and blanket formed a buffer between them that right now she desperately needed because, despite everything, she was still vulnerable. "Let me go," she said quietly. "It's late. We both need sleep."

His dark gaze bored into hers, level and calm. "Come back to bed. We can talk this through."

She fought the familiar magnetic pull, the desire to drop the pillow and blanket and step back into his arms. "No. We can talk in the morning."

A familiar cramping pain low in her stomach pulled Carla out of sleep. A quick trip to the bathroom verified that she had her period and that she was absolutely, positively not pregnant.

Numbly, she walked back to the couch but didn't bother trying to sleep. Until that moment she hadn't realized how much she had desperately needed to be pregnant. If there was a child then there had been the possibility that she could have stayed with Lucas. Now there wasn't one and she had to face reality.

Lucas had broken up with Sophie when she had aborted his child. He had also proposed marriage when he had thought she could be pregnant. For a man who had gone to considerable lengths to cut her out of his life, that was a huge turnaround. She could try fooling herself that it was because he loved her, even if he didn't quite know it, but she couldn't allow herself to think that way. She deserved better.

Now she knew for sure she wasn't pregnant. There were no more excuses.

Her decision made, she opted not to shower, because that would wake Lucas. Instead, she found her gym bag, which was sitting by the kitchen counter and which contained fresh underwear, sweatpants, a tank and a light cotton hoodie. She quickly dressed and laced on sneakers. Her handbag with all her medications was in the bedroom. She couldn't risk getting that, but she had a cash card and some cash tucked in her gym bag. That would give her enough money and the ID she needed to book a flight back to Sydney. She had plenty of medication at home, so leaving the MediPACKs in her purse wasn't a problem. She would collect her handbag along with the rest of her luggage from Lucas when he got back to Sydney.

Working quickly, she jammed toiletries into the sports bag. She paused to listen, but there was no sound or movement from the bedroom. She wrote a brief note on hotel paper, explaining that she was not pregnant and was therefore ending their engagement. She anchored the note to the kitchen counter with the engagement ring.

Picking up the sports bag and hooking her handbag over her shoulder, she quietly let herself out of the room.

Within a disorientingly short period of time the elevator shot her down to the lobby. The speed with which she had walked away from what had been the most important adult relationship of her life made her stomach lurch sickly, but she couldn't go back.

She couldn't afford to commit one more minute to a man who had put more creative effort into cutting her out of his life than he ever had to including her.

A small sound pulled Lucas out of a fitful sleep.

Kicking free of the tangled sheet, he pushed to his feet and pulled on the pair of pants he'd left tossed over the arm of a chair.

Moonlight slanted through shuttered windows as he walked swiftly through the suite. His suspicion that the sound that had woken him had been the closing of the front door turned to certainty when he found a note and Carla's engagement ring on the kitchen counter.

The note was brief. Carla wasn't pregnant. Rather than both of them being pushed into a marriage that clearly had no chance of working, she had decided to give him his out.

She had left him.

Lucas's hand closed on the note, crumpling it. His heart was pounding as if he'd run a race and his chest felt tight. Taking a deep breath, he controlled the burst of raw panic.

He would get her back. He had to.

She loved him, of that fact he was certain. All it would take was the right approach.

He had messed up one too many times. With the double emotional hit of discovering that he had intended to propose to Lilah then the shock of discovering that she wasn't pregnant, he guessed he shouldn't be surprised that she had reacted by running.

Like Sophie.

His stomach clenched at the thought that Carla could have an accident. Then logic reasserted itself. That wouldn't happen. Carla was so *not* like Sophie he didn't know how he could have imagined she was in the first place.

But this time he would not compound his mistake by failing to act. He would make sure that Carla was safe. He would not fail her again.

He loved her.

His stomach clenched as he examined that reality. He couldn't change the past; all he could do was try to change the future.

Sliding the note into his pocket along with the ring, he strode back to his room to finish dressing. He pulled on shoes and found his wallet and watch. The possibility that he could lose Carla struck him anew and for a split second he was almost paralyzed with fear. Until that moment he hadn't understood how necessary Carla was to him.

For more than two years she had occupied his thoughts and haunted his nights. He had thought the affair would run its course; instead his desire had strengthened. In order to control what he had deemed an obsession, he had minimized contact and compartmentalized the affair.

The strategy hadn't worked. The more restrictive he had become in spending time with Carla, the more uncontrollable his desire had become.

She wasn't pregnant.

Until that moment he hadn't known how much he had wanted Carla to be pregnant. Since the out-of-control lovemaking on Medinos, the possibility of a pregnancy had initiated a number of responses from him. The most powerful had been the cast-iron excuse it had provided him to bring her back into his life. But as the days had passed, the thought of Carla losing her taut hourglass shape and growing soft and round with his child had become increasingly appealing. Along with the need to keep Carla tied close, he had wanted to be a father.

Pocketing his keys, he strode out of the suite. Frustration gripped him when he jabbed the elevator call button then had to wait. His gaze locked on the glowing arrow above the doors, and he scraped at his jaw, which harbored a five-o'clock shadow.

Dragging rough fingers through his rumpled hair, he began to pace.

He couldn't lose her.

Whatever it took, he would do it. He would get her back.

He recalled the expression on Carla's face when she had found the engagement ring he had ordered for Lilah, her stricken comment that Constantine had wanted Sienna enough that he had kidnapped her.

Raw emotion gripped him.

Almost the exact opposite of his behaviour.

Carla walked quickly through the lobby, which was empty except for a handful of guests checking out. She had wasted frantic minutes checking the backstage area. It had been empty of possessions, which meant either Elise or Nina had her things.

Too fragile to bear the stirring of interest she would cause by waiting inside, she avoided the concierge desk and made a beeline for the taxi stand.

Not having her medication wasn't ideal. She hadn't taken any last night, and now she would go most of the day without them. Antacids would have to do. She could wait out the short flight to Sydney and the taxi ride home, where there was a supply of pills in her bathroom cupboard.

A pale-faced group of guests, obviously catching an early flight out, were climbing into the only taxi waiting near the hotel entrance. Settling her gym bag down on the dusty pavement, she settled herself to wait for the next taxi to turn into the hotel pickup area.

Long seconds ticked by. She glanced in at the empty reception area, her tension growing, not because she was desperate to escape, she finally admitted to herself, but because a weak part of her still wanted Lucas to stride out and stop her from going.

Not that Lucas was likely to chase her.

Shivering in the faint chill of the air, she stared at the bleak morning sky now graying in the east as a cab finally braked to a halt beside her.

She slipped into the rear seat with her bag, requested the cab driver take her to the airport and gave the hotel entrance one last look before she stared resolutely at the road unfolding ahead.

Why would Lucas come after her, when she was giving him the thing he had always valued most in their relationship, his freedom?

Lucas caught the flash of the taxi's taillights as it turned out of the resort driveway and the panic that had gripped him while he'd endured the slow elevator ride turned to cold fear.

Sliding his phone out of his pocket, he made a series of calls then strode back into the hotel and took the elevator to the rooftop.

Seconds later, Tiberio phoned back. He had obtained Carla's destination from the taxi company. She was headed for Brisbane Airport. He had checked with the flight desk and she had already booked her flight out to Sydney.

The quiet, efficient way Carla had left him hit Lucas forcibly. No threats or manipulation, no smashed crockery or showy exit in a sports car, just a calm, orderly exit with her flight already arranged.

He felt like kicking himself that it had taken him this long to truly see who she was, and to understand why she was so irresistible to him. He hadn't fallen into lust with a second Sophie. He had fallen in love for the first time—with a woman who was smart and fascinating and perfect for him.

Then he had spent the past two years trying to crush what he felt for her.

Issuing a further set of instructions, Lucas settled down to wait.

Carla frowned as the taxi took the wrong exit and turned into a sleepy residential street opposite a sports field. "This isn't the way to the airport."

The driver gave her an odd look in the rearview mirror

and hooked his radio, which he'd been muttering into for the past few minutes, back on its rest. "I have to wait for someone."

Carla started to argue, then the rhythmic chop of rotor blades slicing the air caught her attention. A sleek black helicopter set down on the sports field. A tall, dark-haired man climbed out, ducking his head as he walked beneath the rotor blades.

Her heart slammed in her chest. She had wanted Lucas to come after her. Contrarily, now that he was here, all she wanted to do was run.

Depressing the door handle, she pushed the door wide and groped for the cash in the side pocket of her gym bag. She shoved some money at the driver, more than enough to cover his meter, and dragged the sports bag off the back-seat. A split second later the world flipped sideways and she found herself cradled in Lucas's arms.

Her heart pounded a crazy tattoo. The strap of the sports bag slipped from her fingers as she grabbed at his shoulders. "What do you think you're doing?"

His gaze, masked by dark glasses, seared over her face. "Kidnapping you. That's the benchmark, isn't it?"

Her mouth went dry at his reference to the conversation they'd had when she had listed the things Constantine had done that proved his love for Sienna. Her pulse rate ratcheted up another notch.

She stared into the remote blankness of the dark glasses, suddenly terribly afraid to read too much into his words. "If you're afraid I'm going to do something silly or have an accident, I'm not. I'm just giving you the out you want."

"I know. I read the note." He placed her in the seat directly behind the pilot. "And by the way, here it is."

He took out a piece of the hotel notepaper, tore it into

pieces and tossed it into the downdraft of the blades. The scraps of paper whirled away.

"What are you doing now?" she asked as he started to walk away from the chopper.

The noise muffled his reply. "Getting your shoes and makeup and whatever else it is that makes you happy."

Seconds later, he tossed her sports bag on the floor at her feet and belted himself in beside her.

"Where are we going?" She had to yell now above the noise from the chopper.

Lucas fitted a set of earphones over her head then donned a set himself. "A cabin. In the mountains."

A short flight later the helicopter landed in a clearing. Within minutes the pilot had lifted off, leaving them with a box stamped with the resort's logo on the side. Lucas picked it up. She guessed it was food.

Carla stared at the rugged surrounding range of the Lamingtons, the towering gum trees and silvery gleam of a creek threading through the valley below. "I can't believe you kidnapped me."

"It worked for Constantine."

Her heart pounded at his answer. It wasn't quite a declaration of love, but it was close.

She followed Lucas into the cabin, which was huge. With its architectural angles, sterile planes of glass and comfortable leather couches it was more like an upscale executive palace than her idea of a rustic holiday cottage.

He placed the box on a kitchen counter then began unloading what looked like a picnic lunch. A kidnapping, Atraeus-style, with all the luxury trappings.

Frustrated by his odd mood and the dark glasses, she walked outside, grabbed her sports bag and brought it into the house. She could feel herself floundering, unable to ask the questions that mattered in case the hope that had flared to life when he had bodily picked her up and deposited her in the helicopter was extinguished. "It's not as if this is a real kidnapping."

He stopped, his face curiously still. "How 'real' did you want it to be?"

Sixteen

"We're alone. We're together." Lucas reached for calm when all he really wanted was to pull her close and kiss her.

But that approach hadn't worked so far. Carla had actually tried to run from him, which had altered his game plan somewhat. Plan B was open-ended, meaning he no longer knew what he was doing except that he wasn't going to blow this now by resorting to sex. "We can do what we should have done last night and talk this out. Have you eaten?"

"No." She stared absently at the rich, spicy foods and freshly squeezed juice he had set out then began rummaging through her gym bag just in case there was a stray pack of antacids in one of the pockets.

Lucas, intensely aware of every nuance of expression on Carla's face, tensed when she picked up the phone on the counter. "What's wrong? Who are you calling?"

She frowned when the call wasn't picked up. "Elise. She can get me some medication I need."

"What medication?" But suddenly he knew. The small bag of snacks she carried, her preoccupation with what she was eating and the weight loss. "You're either diabetic or you've got an ulcer."

"The second one."

He could feel his temper soaring. "Why didn't you tell me?"

"You weren't exactly over the moon when I got ill in Thailand."

"You had a virus in Thailand."

"And the viral bacteria just happened to attack an area of my stomach that was still healing from an ulcer I had two years ago. Although I didn't find that out until the ulcer perforated and I got to hospital."

He felt himself go ice-cold inside. "You had a perforated ulcer?" For a split second he thought he must have misheard. "You could have died. Why didn't you tell me?"

Her gaze was cool. "After what happened in Thailand I didn't want you to know I was sick again." She shrugged. "Mom and Sienna didn't know about you, so it was hardly likely they would call you. Why would they? You had no visible role in my life."

That was all going to change, he thought grimly. From now on he was going to be distinctly, in-your-face visible.

He felt like kicking himself. In Thailand he had distanced himself from Carla when she was sick because the enforced intimacy of looking after her had made him want a lot more than the clandestine meetings they'd had through the year. Pale and ill, sweating and shivering, Carla hadn't been either glamorous or sexually desirable. She had simply been *his*.

He had wanted to continue caring for her, wanted to keep her close. But the long hours he had spent sitting beside her bed, waiting for her fever to break, had catapulted him back to his time with Sophie.

He had not wanted her to be that important to him. He hadn't wanted to make himself vulnerable to the kind of guilt and betrayal his relationship with Sophie had resulted in. He could admit that now.

"When was the last time you had your medication?"

She punched in another number. "Lunch, yesterday. That's why I'm calling the resort. Either Nina or Elise can go to the suite and find my handbag, which is where I keep my Medi-PACKs. I'm hoping Tiberio or one of your other bodyguards could drive up with it."

"If you think I'm taking two hours to get you the medication you need, think again." Lucas's cell was already in his hand. He speed dialed and bit out commands in rapid Medinian, hung up and slipped the phone back in his pocket. "Our ride will be here in fifteen minutes."

She slipped her phone back in her handbag. "I could have waited. It's not that bad. I just have to manage my stomach for a few weeks."

"You might be able to wait, but *I* can't. What do you think it did to me to hear that you almost died in hospital?"

"I didn't *almost* die." She grimaced. "Although it wasn't pleasant, that's for sure. It wasn't as if I wasn't used to dealing with the ulcer. It just got out of hand."

He went still inside. "How long did you say you had the ulcer?"

"Two years or so."

Around the time they had met. His jaw tightened at this further evidence of how blind he had been with Carla. He knew ulcers could be caused by a number of factors, but number one was stress. In retrospect, the first time they had made love and he had found out she was a virgin he should have taken a mental step back and reappraised. He hadn't done it. He hadn't wanted to know what might hurt or upset

Carla, or literally eat away at her, because he had been so busy protecting himself.

"News flash," she said with an attempted grin. "I'm a worrier. Can't seem to ditch the habit."

He reached her in two steps and hauled her close. "The woman I love collapses because she has a perforated ulcer," he muttered, "and all you can say is that it *wasn't pleasant?*"

Carla froze in Lucas's arms and, like a switch flicking, she swung from depression and despair to deliriously happy. She stared, riveted by his fierce gaze, and decided she didn't need to pinch herself. "You really do love me?" He had said the words last night but they had felt neutral, empty.

"I love you. Why do you think I couldn't resist you?"

"But it did take you two years to figure that out."

"Don't remind me. Tell me how you ended up with the ulcer."

"Okay, here it goes, but now you might fall out of love with me. I'm a psycho-control-freak-perfectionist. I worked myself into the ground trying to lift Ambrosi's profile and micromanage all of our advertising layouts and pamphlets. When I started color coordinating the computer mouses and mouse pads, Sienna sent me to the family doctor. Jennifer gave me Losec and told me to stop taking everything so seriously, to lighten up and change my life. A week later, I met you."

"And turned my life upside down."

"I wish, but it didn't seem that way." She snuggled in close, unable to stop grinning, loving the way he was staring at her so fiercely. "All I knew was that I was running the relationship in the exact opposite way I wanted, supposedly to avoid stress. If you'd arrived in my life a couple of weeks early, you would have met a different woman."

"I fell in love with you. Instantly."

She closed her eyes and basked for just a few seconds. "Tell me again."

"I love you," he said calmly and, finally, he kissed her.

During the short helicopter ride, Lucas insisted on being given a crash course on her condition. When they reached the doctor's office, which was in a nearby town, Carla took Losec and an antibiotic under the eagle eye of both the doctor and Lucas.

At Lucas's insistence, the doctor also gave her a thorough checkup. Twenty minutes later she was given a clean bill of health.

They exited the office and strolled around to the parking lot to wait for the rental vehicle that Tiberio, apparently, had arranged to have delivered.

Lucas had kept his arm around her waist, keeping her close. "How are you feeling?"

"Fine." She leaned on him slightly. Not that she needed the support, but she loved the way he was treating her, as if she was a piece of precious, delicate porcelain. She could get used to it.

Lucas cupped her face, his fingers tangling in her hair. "I need to explain. To apologize."

Carla listened while Lucas explained about how her illness in Thailand had forced him to confront the guilt and betrayal of the past and had pushed him into a decision to break off with her.

His expression was remote. "But as you know, I couldn't break it off completely. When Constantine told me he was marrying Sienna, I knew I had to act once and for all."

"So you asked Lilah to accompany you to the wedding."

"She was surprised. Before that we had only ever spoken on a business level."

"But she guessed what was going on the night before the wedding."

"Only because she saw us together." He pulled her close, burying his face in her hair. "I'm not proud of what I did but I was desperate. I didn't realize I was in love with you until I read the note you left in the hotel room and discovered that you had left me. It was almost too late."

He hugged her close for long minutes, as if he truly did not want to let her go. "I've wasted a lot of time. Two years."

"There were good reasons we couldn't be together in the beginning. Some of those reasons were mine."

He frowned. "Reasons that suited me."

Gripping her hands gently in his, he went down on one knee. "Carla Ambrosi, will you marry me and be the love of my life for the rest of my life?"

He reached into his pocket and produced the sky-blue diamond ring, which he must have been carrying with him all along, and gently slipped it on the third finger of her left hand.

Tears blurred Carla's eyes at the soft gleam in Lucas's gaze, the intensity of purpose that informed her that if she said no he would keep on asking until she was his.

Emotion shimmered through her, settled in her heart, because she *had* been his all along.

"Yes," she said, the answer as simple as the kiss that followed, the long minutes spent holding each other and the promise of a lifetime together.

* * * * *

REQUEST YOUR FREE BOOKS!
2 FREE NOVELS PLUS 2 FREE GIFTS!

Harlequin *Desire*

ALWAYS POWERFUL, PASSIONATE AND PROVOCATIVE

YES! Please send me 2 FREE Harlequin Desire® novels and my 2 FREE gifts (gifts are worth about $10). After receiving them, if I don't wish to receive any more books, I can return the shipping statement marked "cancel." If I don't cancel, I will receive 6 brand-new novels every month and be billed just $4.30 per book in the U.S. or $4.99 per book in Canada. That's a saving of at least 14% off the cover price! It's quite a bargain! Shipping and handling is just 50¢ per book in the U.S. and 75¢ per book in Canada.* I understand that accepting the 2 free books and gifts places me under no obligation to buy anything. I can always return a shipment and cancel at any time. Even if I never buy another book, the two free books and gifts are mine to keep forever.

225/326 HDN FEF3

Name	(PLEASE PRINT)	
Address		Apt. #
City	State/Prov.	Zip/Postal Code

Signature (if under 18, a parent or guardian must sign)

Mail to the **Reader Service:**
IN U.S.A.: P.O. Box 1867, Buffalo, NY 14240-1867
IN CANADA: P.O. Box 609, Fort Erie, Ontario L2A 5X3

Not valid for current subscribers to Harlequin Desire books.

Want to try two free books from another line?
Call 1-800-873-8635 or visit www.ReaderService.com.

* Terms and prices subject to change without notice. Prices do not include applicable taxes. Sales tax applicable in N.Y. Canadian residents will be charged applicable taxes. Offer not valid in Quebec. This offer is limited to one order per household. All orders subject to credit approval. Credit or debit balances in a customer's account(s) may be offset by any other outstanding balance owed by or to the customer. Please allow 4 to 6 weeks for delivery. Offer available while quantities last.

Your Privacy—The Reader Service is committed to protecting your privacy. Our Privacy Policy is available online at www.ReaderService.com or upon request from the Reader Service.

We make a portion of our mailing list available to reputable third parties that offer products we believe may interest you. If you prefer that we not exchange your name with third parties, or if you wish to clarify or modify your communication preferences, please visit us at www.ReaderService.com/consumerschoice or write to us at Reader Service Preference Service, P.O. Box 9062, Buffalo, NY 14269. Include your complete name and address.

HDES11B

New York Times *and* USA TODAY *bestselling author Vicki Lewis Thompson returns with yet another irresistible cowpoke! Meet Mathew Tredway—cowboy, horse whisperer and honorary Son of Chance.*

Read on for a sneak peek from the bestselling miniseries SONS OF CHANCE:

LEAD ME HOME
Available July 2012 only from Harlequin® Blaze™.

AS MATTHEW RETURNED to the corral and Houdini, the taste of Aurelia's mouth was on his lips and her scent clung to his clothes. He'd briefly satisfied the craving growing within him, and like a light snack before a meal, it would have to do.

When he'd first walked into the kitchen, his mind had been occupied with the challenge of training Houdini. He'd thought his concentration would hold long enough to get some carrots, ask about the corn bread and leave before succumbing to Aurelia's appeal. He'd miscalculated. Within a very short time, desire had claimed every brain cell.

Although seducing her this morning was out of the question, his libido had demanded some sort of satisfaction. He'd tried to deny that urge and had nearly made it out of the house. Apparently his willpower was no match for the temptation of Aurelia's mouth, though, and he'd turned around.

If he'd ever felt this kind of desperate need for a woman, he couldn't recall it. During the night, as he'd lain in his narrow bunk listening to the cowhands snore, he'd searched for an explanation as to why Aurelia affected him this way.

Sometime in the early-morning hours he'd come up with

the answer. After years of dating women who were rolling stones like he was, he'd developed an itch for a hearth-and-home kind of woman. Aurelia, with her cooking skills and voluptuous body, could give him that.

With luck, once he'd scratched this particular itch, he'd be fine again. He certainly hoped so, because he had no intention of giving up his career, and travel was a built-in requirement. Plus he liked to travel and had no real desire to stay in one spot and become domesticated.

Tonight he'd say all that to Aurelia, because he didn't want her going into this with any illusions about permanence. He figured that when the right guy came along, she'd get married and have kids.

Too bad that guy wouldn't be him....

Will Aurelia be the one to corral this cowboy for good?
Find out in: LEAD ME HOME

Available July 2012
wherever Harlequin® Blaze™ books are sold.

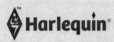
Harlequin®

n o c t u r n e™

Take a bite out of summer!

Enjoy three tantalizing tales from
Harlequin® Nocturne™ fan-favorite authors

MICHELE HAUF,
Kendra Leigh Castle
and Lisa Childs

VACATION
WITH A VAMPIRE

Available July 2012!
Wherever books are sold.